A Royal Mind

Abi Black

The Author:

Abigail believes in the power of a good book. A good book can take readers of any age on an adventure that will stay with them forever. That is the goal she has for her books, to provide a lasting adventure. Her inspiration stems from reading Ella Enchanted over and over again until the pages started falling apart, and of course traveling through the wardrobe into Narnia age after age. During the day she's teaching 7th graders, but after the bell rings she's crocheting, reading fantasy, scanning through Pinterest, and drinking coffee.

A Royal Mind

The Legend of Ignis

by

Abi Black

Bumgardner Publishing- Barboursville, WV

2. Edition, 2023

© May All rights reserved.

Bumgardner Publishing- Barboursville, WV
abielizblack@gmail.com

Table of Contents

quietly out of the closet and into her seat as if she had been there the whole time. It usually worked.

Today, however, it did not.

When she slipped out of the closet, she stayed unnoticed by the teacher and most of the students, but as she slid into her seat with a sigh of relief, she heard a cough behind her.

"Aster, so glad you could join us today," said a familiar voice behind her.

Aster gulped. Her heart plummeted into her stomach, and she tensed her shoulders, knowing the trouble that was about to come down on her. She turned around and tried to look innocently at the headmaster standing stoically behind her. Headmaster Roark was not unkind, but his dark eyes and constant moody expression made the students respect him from a distance.

"Hello, Headmaster. I've been here. I was just taking some time for quiet reflection inside the closet to give my full attention to my lessons."

It was a weak excuse, and Aster knew he wasn't buying it, but she didn't want to come out and admit she was late again. The headmaster gave her a firm look and pointed to the door. Aster knew what that meant. She sighed, grabbed her things, and walked to the door, trailed by the mutterings of her classmates. She looked at them and rolled her eyes. They thought they were so much better than her, but at least she had a personality. Her classmates were a dull group who didn't have a curious bone in their bodies; therefore they neither understood her, nor did she understand them.

Professor Andromeda gave her the disappointed look Aster expected, but Aster shrugged her shoulders, as if to say, *"Are you surprised?"*

The headmaster lead Aster down the corridors, toward his office, a route she knew well. They entered his stoic office, and he motioned for her to sit in the chair across from his desk. She knew the routine. He'd reprimand her for being late, remind her good students are on time, it's disrespectful to teachers to be late, etc.

Chapter 1

Aster jolted up out of a deep sleep, almost falling out of her chair. She'd been having a wonderful dream, the same dream about beautiful, rolling hills of green with a clear blue lake flowing into a small river that seemed to never end. But every time she'd had the dream, it ended with the beautiful land being destroyed by a dark storm, screams echoing in the emptiness. She moaned with exhaustion as the early morning light streamed in from the window behind her.

Aster blinked stretching the kink in her back and neck and leaning back in her comfortable chair, when she suddenly remembered what day, it was. "Not again," she mumbled. She had unknowingly fallen asleep in their family library on a school night. Something she often did which frustrated her parents. She stood up and stretched her aching limbs. Heading for the door, she tripped over a stack of books she'd left near the hearth. She reached out, grasping desperately at the shelf in front of her to keep from falling. Her hands caught on a book, but the book didn't fall out of the shelf; instead, it stuck out halfway, and a loud *pop* sounded, as if something broke apart from behind the shelf. Aster's stomach plummeted, picturing her parents' reaction to her breaking something, again. To her relief, the shelf remained intact, but relief soon turned to confusion. She watched in awe as the entire shelf swung open like a door, revealing a hidden room with a narrow stone-spiral staircase. The room was small, just an alcove really. Aster noticed an old trunk layered with dust against the wall next to the stairs.

"Don't go looking into places and things that aren't yours," her mother had told her once, but her mind whirled with ideas, and as usual, her curiosity won out. She forgot about school and went to open the

trunk. Its owner had left it unlocked, and she opened the creaking lid to explore its contents. She found old baby clothes, family pictures, and old books. Wedged between the books, a red leather journal caught her eye. The journal looked quite old, even with the dust wiped off it. It had no special design or name printed on the front, just a symbol on the spine that looked like a fire, tied up in knots. She opened the journal and thumbed through the pages. Her eyes stopped on a page written in an unfamiliar language. Despite being a bright student overall, Aster struggled with languages. She tried deciphering the page, but the only word she understood was *Intrusus*. With her limited knowledge she understood the word to mean "Intruder."

She wondered if this page concerned the storms that had been wreaking havoc across the three lands, the ones many people called the "Intrusions." The dark storms enveloped towns, either with rain, fire, or floods, and afterward, when the dust settled, the towns had been completely wiped out. Not a trace of debris left. It was as if they'd just vanished in the storm. Though few survived, the ones who did had to find a new home, intruding upon others lands, and claiming them as their own.

The Intrusions had started on the outskirts of each of the three lands and were working their way inland, slowly but surely, swallowing everything up in utter darkness. Aster had once heard her parents arguing over their safety in Verd, a small town in the middle of Veridi. Her father told her mother they didn't have to worry, they were too far inland, and the Evanders would stop the Intrusions. Aster wasn't sure what to believe, though. She didn't quite trust the ruling hands of the Evanders. They were the ruling body over the three lands, Veridi, Vela, and Gemma, but never once did they seem to care about the plight of the people.

"Aster!"

Aster heard sister calling her name. She quickly shut the trunk, tucked the journal under her arm, and darted out of the room, closing the hidden door before her sister could see.

Her younger sister, Amity, poked her red head into the library, frowning at her.

"You did it again, didn't you? What was it this time? Some great new story or invention pop inside your head?" she grumbled. Aster pushed past her, ignoring Amity's jab. No one in her family understood her or her love of reading, discovery, and daydreaming.

"How late is it?" Aster asked, pulling her school dress out of her armoire.

"Late," Amity stated. "We have to leave for school in less than ten minutes."

"I'll be ready in five," Aster smarted back.

"No one would ever know you're the oldest by the way you act."

Aster noticed the immense disapproval on her sister's face. Aster knew she was right, though. Despite Aster being eighteen years old compared to Amity's fourteen, her younger sister often treated her like a child because of her unique qualities. Even their parents remarked on how Aster's daydreams were childish things she needed to give up, but try as she might, she couldn't stop.

Aster hoped she could accomplish getting ready in five minutes, but she knew she'd have no help from her sister. Aster hated running late, though today more than others, because she wanted to ask her mother about the journal she'd found. It held many fascinating and confusing things, and something inside her said the pages held a deep secret.

"Aster, what are you doing?" her mother cried, interrupting her thoughts. Aster realized she was sitting on her bed, mindlessly fingering her hair. She must have drifted off in a daydream as she was getting ready for school.

"Sorry, Mother! I'm ready. I really was trying to do better." Her mother sighed and shook her head as Aster fixed her sleep-matted braid into a bun on top of her head and stuffed her feet into her brown leather boots. She glanced in the mirror and grimaced at how her deep red hair looked like a tangled bird's nest just waiting for a robin to lay its eggs.

"Aster, I-" her mother started to say, but Aster stopped her.

"I know, Mother, I need to be ready for school on time, and not allow myself to get so distracted. I know I need to prepare and be more like Amity and-" She felt herself starting to lose it before her mother put a hand up to stop her flood of words.

"I was going to say, I made your lunch and it's by the door. I don't want you to be like anyone but yourself, but you do need to work on not allowing yourself to become so distracted you forget about what's happening right in front of you."

Aster's mother put a gentle hand on her face, and Aster ducked her head, feeling guilty for her outburst, and grateful for her mother.

"Thank you," Aster said giving her a quick kiss on the cheek before darting down the steps to leave.

She grabbed her coat, pulling one arm through while grabbing the lunch bag her mother left by the door.

"Be careful!" her mother shouted from the top of the stairs. Aster nodded, the lunch bag in her mouth as she put her other arm in her coat. As she ran out the door, she made a mental note to make it home in time for dinner, maybe even with enough time to help Mother make it and set the table! Now, wouldn't that surprise everyone!

She ran quickly, heading for the shortcut through the woods, her heart pounding out of her chest. She gasped as a stitch caught in her side but didn't stop. She couldn't be late for school again. Her mother would give her a tongue-lashing, and her father would look at her with his disapproving eyes. Neither of those occurrences was rare for Aster. Out of all her family, she was the problem, the black sheep. She wished she could follow the rules, wished she could control her thoughts and not fall into daydreaming. Her daydreams always got her into trouble. They caused her to forget her surroundings, sometimes fall, almost step in front of a moving carriage, or, as today, be late for school. Her mother's words played inside her head: *"Aster!*

You need to keep your eyes on what's in front of you, not up in the clouds. You'll only fall down once you realize the clouds can't hold you."

But she didn't agree with her mother. Her clouds held her up just fine. She solved most of her problems and discovered new things through her time in the clouds. Through books she learned about places far away, animals and people she'd never seen, things she never would have discovered if it hadn't been for books. She'd become curious about something she'd seen, heard, or read, then off she'd float, up into the clouds, daydreaming. Her parents or teachers often brought her down with their sharp voices, blowing away the clouds and causing her to fall roughly back to Earth. She didn't like when they did that, especially when she was just on the verge of a breakthrough or in a vivid dream. It always took effort to find the thought again or remember how she reached her breakthrough.

Even now, she had to fight against floating off up into the clouds. She had to focus if she was going to make it to school on time. Just ahead was the clearing, leading to an open hole in the back wall of the city, conveniently situated behind the school. The wall was old and had fallen into disrepair, but this part was on the edge of the woods, so they didn't see a need to fix it. It had therefore become Aster's way of sneaking into school when she was late.

Breaking through the trees, she came out panting. The air was filled with a loud ringing, and her stomach dropped as the last bell before the school day started. She ran toward the hole in the wall, looking around for any roaming village guards, patrolling the area. Seeing none in sight, she stealthily pulled herself up on the handholds she had created and propelled herself through the hole into the city. The back door of the school was just ahead, a few more feet. She was almost within reach when some force suddenly pulled her back, causing her to stumble.

She screamed.

A guard must have been waiting in a blind spot and now had a hold of her shoulder, looking sternly down at her.

"Late again, Aster," Josiah said.

Aster sighed in relief. Josiah was one of the younger guards and often went easy on her. He also rarely treated her like she was crazy for daydreaming.

She grinned. "Josiah, good morning," she said, trying to sound as innocent as possible. "You know I wouldn't be late if it weren't for a good reason."

He scoffed at her attempt to get away with her tardiness. "Oh, I'm sure. What glorious discovery have you had this morning?"

She smiled. "It was my best yet," she said, her voice rising with excitement. He'd opened her a chance to tell someone who would at least feign interest, and she would not miss it.

"I found an old book in our library, and I began reading through it. The pages contain history and some old journal entries, but then I came across a section I couldn't read. It's not in any language I've ever seen or heard of, but it's old, and that makes it important. It could say anything!"

Josiah looked at her with doubt and confusion, looks she often received after telling of her curiosities. "Another language, huh? And what makes you think it couldn't just be someone's list of farm equipment or boring notes about weather and crops?"

She rolled her eyes. Sometimes she felt like the only one with an imagination around here. "I know because I could make out a meaning for one word, *Intrusus*, which if I'm right, means someone entering inside, possibly an intruder. But the most curious part is that the 'I' is capitalized, like a name..."

"Stop!" Josiah interrupted. His face changed almost instantly, his laughing eyes turning wide and his mouth shutting tightly, curving in a frown, as his broad shoulders tensed under his uniform. He glanced around with frantic eyes to see if anyone had heard Aster's outburst.

Aster's knees buckled under Josiah's hand as he pressed down harder on her shoulder.

"Josiah, stop! What did I say?" She had never seen Josiah react like this, and it scared her.

He released her shoulder. "Nothing," he said, having to intentionally untense his muscles and force a small smile, as though trying to calm himself.

"Forget it," he said. "And forget what you think you read. Put the book back on the shelf and don't look at it again. Don't tell anyone else what you read or that you found it at all."

He released her shoulder and stepped back. "Now, go inside to class and tell your teacher I asked you to help me, and that's why you're late."

Aster stood stunned as Josiah stalked off. She did not know what had just happened, and Josiah's instructions to "forget it" had only piqued her interest even more. There was no way she would forget, and now she felt sure there was some deeper meaning to this journal. Though, how Josiah knew anything about it was beyond her. It just added to her growing curiosity. There was no doubt in her mind now; she had to find the meaning of the journal.

Chapter 2

Aster snapped herself out of the clouds and rushed to the hidden entrance. She carefully made her way through the secret passageway, trying to focus and not think about her strange encounter with Josiah. She walked through the tight, hidden corridor that led to a closet in Professor Andromeda's classroom.

Her favorite teacher, Professor Andromeda, was one of the few who understood and respected Aster's daydreams and curious questions. Aster would stay behind after class and discuss things from the lesson that interested her and elements she wanted to understand better. After school, Aster would often help Professor Andromeda clean up her classroom, and they'd walk home together since the professor's small house was on the way to Aster's. Aster not only loved talking but hearing her professor's stories of her home. Andromeda was from Vela, the neighboring land off the shores of Toparius, the former capital of Veridi. Aster loved hearing about the beaches of Vela and the beautiful blue ocean. Andromeda's dark skin and long, dark braided hair made her stand out in the small town of Verd, but so did her engaging personality. She was always telling Aster that the only way to change the impossible was to dream it's possible. She tried to help Aster reign in her dreams, to lessen her reprimands at home and school, but she never discouraged them entirely.

Aster felt a prick of guilt, because she knew her late arrival would disappoint Professor Andromeda, though not as much as other teachers.

She reached the end of the passageway and looked through the crack in the door. She could see the backs of the students and the professor facing them from the front of the room. All she had to do was wait until Professor Andromeda turned her back, then Aster would do what she had done many times before and slip

"Aster," the headmaster said, "you aren't like the other students, are you?"

Aster looked at him in surprise. What is that supposed to mean? she wondered. She did not know where this line of questioning was going. Did he mean that as a good thing or not—that she wasn't like the other students? Something about his attitude toward was different today. It wasn't news to her that she was different, but the headmaster had never talked to her like this—less like a child and more like a peer, like how Professor Andromeda treated her.

He didn't let her answer. "You might be curious about how I knew to wait for your stealthy, late entrance. It might surprise you I had a conversation with Josiah, the guard, and he informed me of your late arrival."

Aster scowled at the ground. She thought she could trust Josiah, and why of all times did he betray her now?

He had often caught her being late and never said a word.

The headmaster continued, "He said you were going on about a journal you found and some curiosities inside it that caused you to be late. Curiosities that, if mentioned to anyone else, would have resulted in a much different meeting for you right now."

Aster's questions and curiosity were pounding inside her head. Her heart was racing, and the excitement she felt finding the journal this morning returned, this time with an added mix of dread. What had she done wrong? What was it about this journal that had caused Josiah to betray her—and for the headmaster to be speaking with a tone of warning?

"Headmaster, I don't know what Josiah told you, but it's just a journal that I found in our family library. I don't know what anything inside it means."

He remained quiet, taking in her words, contemplating, and weighing them carefully. Aster waited anxiously and impatiently until he finally spoke again, looking carefully at her reaction to his next words.

"That's not entirely true, though, is it?" Her heart thudded against her chest. How did he know?

How did he know she had already been discerning and cyphering the strange journal and what *Intrusus* might mean? Fear kept her mouth closed tightly.

He seemed to take her silence as confirmation, and he smiled knowingly, looking off into the distance, as if trying to see something that was just beyond his reach.

"That's what I thought," he said with a slight smile. "Thankfully, you gave this information to Josiah, and another guard was not your outlet. He caught me in time this morning and warned me. Professor Andromeda will be glad to know she was right about you," he added in an offhand tone. He seemed to be off in his own world, away from his office, and Aster just sat there, listening as he muttered to himself.

Finally, she could hold her questions no longer. "Headmaster, what is going on?" she entreated. "I don't understand what you're saying. What is wrong with the journal? And why would Josiah feel the need to tell you? And why would it have been bad if I had told another guard?"

She said all of this quickly and took a deep breath after the questions flew out of her mouth.

The headmaster looked at her with a direct, inquisitive stare. Aster looked straight back at him, attempting to match his stare. She had just as many questions as he had answers. He finally looked away, and Aster was glad, for her resolve was waning, but she didn't want to be the first to break eye contact.

A knock sounded on the door, startling Aster. She stared in surprise as Professor Andromeda walked through the door.

"Perfect timing." the headmaster said.

"I left the other students reading; they didn't seem suspicious."

"No, I didn't think they would. Aster, show Professor Andromeda what you found this morning in your family library."

She often confided in Professor Andromeda, but now she felt torn. What was happening here? Could she trust the headmaster? Was he telling her the truth, that she had stumbled upon something potentially dangerous yet terribly mysterious and exciting at the same time? Hesitantly, she reached into her satchel and pulled out the journal. The red leather burned against her skin with its mounting secrets.

"I knew it," Andromeda breathed.

Aster noticed even the headmaster's eyes were wide with excitement.

"Roark, it's time. It's past time, really. We have to tell her."

"I know-but I don't think it's safe to tell her here. We could wait until.-"

"Tell me what?!" Aster interrupted. She hated when people talked like she wasn't in the room.

"I'm sorry, Aster," Andromeda said. She sat on the edge of the headmaster's desk. "We've waited so long for confirmation, and now you bring it to us on a silver platter. Where should we start, Roark?"

"You're the history teacher, Andi, you begin."

Roark rose from his chair and paced behind his desk, staring out the window, as if keeping watch.

"Aster, that journal is one of many kept and curated by a group of people called Light Keepers. Now, what do you know about the Legend of Ignis?"

"The Legend of Ignis?" Aster repeated. "You mean the bedtime story? Of course, I know it. What does any of this have to do with the Legend of Ignis?"

"Our world wasn't always like it is now," Professor Andromeda answered. "It was full of harmony, full of light, full of love. Your history books have taught you about the three lands."

Aster nodded. She knew the history, and she had read many books about her home, Veridi, with its natural wonders, about Gemma and its giant mountains, and of course, Vela's beautiful sandy beaches and blue waters.

"What your history books don't tell you," Andromeda continued, "is the three lands used to be something beautiful. Once, they formed one large country called Ignis. Three lands joined together by the Central Kingdom, until an enormous earthquake, caused by a life-altering mistake, separated them. The Central Kingdom disappeared and Ignis was split into the lands we know today.

Before the earthquake, the people of Ignis lived in harmony under the rule of a wonderful king. He wasn't harsh or demanding. In fact, he had only one rule for his people, which had to do with a very special book in his library. The only ones allowed to even touch it were the King and his trusted Knight."

"But Professor Andromeda, all of that is just legend. Right?" Aster interrupted, feeling the foundations of everything she thought she knew tremble.

"It's no legend," Professor Andromeda said seriously. "It's all real. I suppose I should explain about the Knight before telling of the tragedy," she mused. "You know only the parts that have been passed around through children's stories, but there's so much more. The Knight was the King's right-hand man. He was like a son to him, and some even say he was, but he didn't want to be treated differently because of his royal blood. Whether or not he was the King's son, the King trusted him to help protect the kingdom and its people. He would have died for the people if necessary, and sadly that's what many thinks happened to him.

He left the Kingdom one night. No one knew where he went, he was just gone. Some thought the Knight must have had an urgent matter to attend to, but the strange part is, he never returned. The Knight loved the people; he loved the Kingdom with his whole heart. That's why he gifted some with special abilities, powers they passed down through generations. He gave them the name Light Keepers. He knew all the people by name, he talked to them, helped them when they were in need, and he always stopped by to join in the celebrations. The people didn't understand why he would abandon them."

Andromeda paused and took a breath.

"Now, here's where my knowledge of the story grows vague. Roark has studied the next part more than I have."

Roark sighed but nodded his assent. Aster saw a shadow of shame sweep across his face. The room felt quiet as a tomb, and Aster played with the hem of her sleeve, feeling increasingly uncomfortable in the silence. The curiosity ate at her. She had to know the next part of the story.

Roark picked up the where Andromeda had left off.

"Years passed, to where the people who witnessed all of this had children and their children had children. No one passed on the story about the unrest, which was wrong of the historians," he added passionately.

"They should have been more prepared. But the only place they recorded it was in the history books in the King's library. The library is where everything fell apart..." Roark trailed off.

"The people loved the library. They saw it as a place they could come find shelter, find wisdom in between pages of books—some written by the King himself, others written by scholars of the past—and of course, the King's Book sat in the middle of the library in a glass case. Only the Librarian Guards held a key to the case, a sign of the King's trust in them. He trusted they would keep it safe, that they wouldn't open it. Then one night, two guards, a husband and wife, were watching over the library, as on any other night, until the Intruder came in and deceived them."

"Intruder! Is that what started the storms?" Aster gasped, completely on the edge of her seat now, drawn into the story like a moth to flame. *Intruder* was the word she'd seen in the journal! However, the headmaster's severe glance made her regret her outburst.

"Sorry," she mumbled.

He turned back to the window, ignoring her apology. "Yes, the Intruder ushered in the dark storms. He deceived the wife first. She fell for his lies, and not only did she open the book, but she read it. Then her husband felt obligated to read it, so as not to leave the burden solely on her. Their actions set off the Intruder's dark curse, the storms. He had significant powers—not as powerful as the King, but enough power to cause immense damage."

Roark's face clouded.

"The King knew the moment it happened, but he wanted Gaia and Tarron, the two guards, to come to him and confess. Instead, they tried to hide their mistake. However, the Intruder did not escape without punishment, forced to live a life of low poverty and exile. The King cursed the Intruder to look like the monster he truly was, and anyone who followed him then or would ever follow him in the future would be cursed as well.

Sadly, his curse, his darkness, had already spread through the kingdom the moment Gaia opened the book. The King banished Gaia and Tarron,. He allowed them and those loyal to him to escape before a devestating earthquake separeted the Central Kingdom from the rest of Ignis. He gave them the lands outside the kingdom as their own to cultivate and grow, and to pass down through their family. Even after their betrayal, he cared about them."

Roark paused, becoming distracted by something happening on the streets below. Aster used this moment to clarify, "So, what happened to the Intruder?"

Roark turned back to face them. "That's a question no one has answered. There's not even a record of his name. He's only ever called the 'Intruder.'"

"Which is why they call the storms Intrusions?" Aster asked. Roark nodded.

"Yes, though the Evanders would never admit it," he said bitterly.

Aster's mind kept reeling with each addition of information. She also vaguely recalled Roark had just mentioned the Intruder had powers.

But what kind of powers? she thought to herself.

Aster pondered the many questions yet to be answered by Roark's story.

"You said Ignis used to be one land instead of split into three—how does this have to do with their separation?"

Professor Andromeda answered this question. "The King may have been able to curse the Intruder, but the Intruder had one more trick up his sleeve. He used his powers to create an earthquake, and the lands split into the three we know today. Gaia and Tarron survived, as did many others who were loyal to the King."

"And the Central Kingdom?" Aster asked with bated breath.

Andromeda's eyes pooled with tears. "Some say it fell into the ocean. Others say a storm, like the Intrusions, swallowed it up. Either way, it's lost to us. Unless…"

"Unless what?" Aster whispered.

Professor Andromeda looked down at her hands before answering. "Unless we can find the Knight. And Aster, only Light Keepers can find him…. Light Keepers are also the only ones who would be able to interpret the word *Intrusus*."

"So," Aster mused, "you need my journal because it might have information useful to find the Knight?"

Andromeda didn't answer right away. Aster watched her glance at Roark, before finally answering.

Andromeda got off Roark's desk and kneeled in front of Aster. "I know this is a lot to throw on you at once. But time is of the essence. Aster, I know you've always struggled with feeling different, but right now, the fate of Ignis rests partly on your being different."

Aster heard her professor's voice, but it sounded far away, like an echo. She pushed herself up out of the chair and away from the other two. She went over to the window and stared at the street below.

"You think I am a… what did you call it? A Light Keeper…? And you want me to find a Knight who disappeared centuries ago so he can reunite a kingdom destroyed by an earthquake? I don't think even my imagination could dreamup something like that."

She watched a crowd of men on the streets below in black clothing, standing in a group and pointing back to the school. One of the men moved his coat back to look at his pocket watch and Aster gasped when she saw the symbol on his vest. It was the symbol of the ruling body of Ignis, the Evanders. Here in Verd. It was never a good sign when they came to town. The pocket-watch man glanced up at the window, but Aster couldn't look away. Her instincts told her to hide, but her body felt frozen in place. Something in the man's face captivated her, but it wasn't because his features were appealing; there was something sinister under his guise of innocence. This was a man pretending to be something he wasn't. She felt herself falling into one of her daydreams, like a strong river current pulling her down against her will.

Aster, wake up!

Aster nearly jumped out of her seat as a voice called her name.

"Aster, what's wrong?" Professor Andromeda came rushing to her as concern spread across her face.

"What's happening down there?" Aster asked.

Andromeda glanced down, and Aster knew from her wide eyes something was wrong.

"Roark, look!" Andromeda said.

Roark rushed over to the window and Aster watched as his usually emotionless face cracked in fear.

"Andi, come on, we have to leave." Roark barked. "Aster, I'm sorry but you're going to have to come with us. You're not safe here."

"Why am I not safe here? Why are the Evanders here?"

Roark hurried to grab papers off his desk and stuffed them into a rough-looking satchel Andromeda had thrown him. They moved in tandem, grabbing a few books from the shelves and a roll of maps, giving Aster the sense, they had done this before.

"The Evanders don't like the idea of a united Ignis or Light Keepers. The minute they get a whiff of such talk, they rush to extinguish it. I'm guessing someone overheard your conversation with Josiah this morning."

Aster cursed her own stupid, reckless mouth.

Professor Andromeda rushed to the large cabinet in the corner behind Aster, which Aster had always thought held only coats and old school robes, but Andi pushed these aside to reveal a wooden door. Aster recognized what it was immediately; it was like the one she had climbed through this morning, back when she thought the most exciting thing in her life was sneaking into class late. Andromeda took a key from around her neck and unlocked it, then pulled the heavy wooden door open. She whipped around and motioned for Aster to follow.

"Hurry, Aster, we have little time. I'm truly sorry for this hurried depature. This isn't at all how I wanted this to go."

Aster felt glued to the spot, but Roark wasn't giving her any more time to decide. He came around his desk, grabbed her arm, and led her to Andromeda. Andromeda helped Aster more gently, and before she knew what was going on, Aster found herself in a dark passage, with the only light coming from the open-door Andromeda still held for Roark to follow.

He didn't.

"Andi, go, now. I'll stay behind and ward off any suspicion," Roark stated firmly, handing her his satchel. Andromeda grabbed his arm instead of the satchel he held out and forced him to look her in the eyes.

"Roark, don't you dare. You know the promise you made, and you know I made the same. Besides, it wouldn't matter if you stayed behind. They would still come looking for us. And we can't do this without you. I can't do this without you," she added quietly.

Roark stared at Professor Andromeda. Aster turned her head, not wanting to intrude on what was apparently a private moment between them. She only glanced back when she heard Roark shut the door. Aster wondered silently to herself what kind of promise they'd made to each other that made him obey her so readily.

Roark lit a lantern he'd grabbed from his desk, and Aster stepped aside so he could lead them through the darkness ahead. She knew little about what has happening, but she knew at this rate she was going to be late for dinner.

Roark led them through the dark tunnel, Aster followed, and Andromeda took up the rear. Explosion-like sounds could be heard and felt as they made their escape, and each time, Aster jumped. She couldn't bring herself to ask who exactly was after them, but she knew it wasn't good, and her mind concocted images of what it would be like when they finally made it outside; none of the images were comforting. She tried focusing on the bobbing light in front of her, but she suddenly felt like the walls were closing in on her, and she felt panic register. Andi noticed and gave her shoulder a squeeze.

"It's okay, Aster. Everything's going to be okay," she said soothingly.

Aster tried to believe her, but the darkness and the unknown didn't help. After what felt like forever, they finally came to a fork in the tunnel-the stone floor continued off to the right while the left diverged on a worn dirt floor. Roark paused for just a second before choosing the path off to the right.

"This should lead us outside," he said.

Aster hesitated. "Wait, this leads outside?"

Roark turned around with an air of frustration. "Yes, we have to get out of the school and into the woods. Josiah will be waiting for us in a pre-arranged location. Now come ,we need to hurry."

But Aster dug her feet in. "What if the Evanders and the town guards are waiting to ambush us?"

Roark sighed. "Aster, I need you to trust me. I've been doing this long enough that I know when it could be a possibility, and this isn't one of those times."

Andromeda gave Aster's hand a squeeze. "It's okay, Aster, you can trust Roark. He's right, we have to keep going, we have to get out of the school."

Aster wanted to trust him, she wanted to trust them both, but she was being made to trust in a lot of unknowns all at once. However, she knew she had no other choice but to follow Roark, who hadn't waited around but continued forward. The three walked in silence until coming to a dead end. Now Aster felt more confused, and somewhat angry as fear set in and the feeling of claustrophobia threatened to engulf her. Before she had time to ask what they were going to do, since Roark had obviously chosen the wrong path, Roark turned, handed the lantern to Andromeda, turned back around, and took a step forward, disappearing into the black abyss. Aster gasped and swung around to face Andi, who didn't seem fazed at all, watching Roark disappear into the darkness. She simply pushed Aster forward and pointed to the space between them and the earthen wall. What Aster hadn't noticed, in her shock at facing a dead-end, was a large hole sloping down and falling into a dark abyss. Professor Andromeda gave her another nudge, but Aster dug her heels into the ground. She refused to budge.

"It's okay, Aster," Professor Andromeda assured her. "You can ease yourself down onto the slide instead of hopping down like he did. He can be such a show-off sometimes." She laughed, trying to lighten the mood.

Aster did not feel like laughing, given the current situation. She glanced down at the slide again, but her feet stayed frozen in place as her nerves bounced all over. She shook her head and backed up straight into Professor Andromeda.

"No, no, you don't. Go down, Aster, it's the only way out, and we're running out of time."

"No, you don't understand, Professor, I can't. I hate small spaces. Especially dark, small spaces. I can't. I can't do it!"

She tried pushing past her, not even sure where she would go, but Professor Andromeda just sighed, and with surprising strength turned Aster around, and pushed her down the dark hole.

Aster didn't even have time to scream. All that came out was a quick gasp as the air rushed out from her and the ground fell beneath her feet as she slid down the hard-packed earthen slide. It felt like she was falling for forever, the rough earth bumping harshly against her spine. Aster finally tumbled out at the bottom, into complete and utter darkness. She laid on the dirt floor in a heap, taken over by shock and fear, when a pair of firm hands grabbed her by the waist and pulled her up. She almost screamed.

"Shh-Aster, it's me, you're fine," Roark said quickly.

Professor Andromeda came down a moment later, and Aster noticed she did it with much more grace than Aster had.

"Now, let's get out of here," Roark instructed. "Andi, I'm going to go up first, and I'll throw the rope down to help you all up when I know it's safe."

He headed for the far wall and brushed away layers of dirt covering footholds in the wall. Carefully, he began climbing towards the rock ledge at the top. Once Roark reached the rock, he steadied himself on the wall and pushed the stone away, allowing light from the outside to stream down on them. For the first time since she had entered the dark tunnel through the office, Aster's shoulders relaxed. Professor Andromeda had seemed so sure they didn't have to worry about a surprise attack, but now, in the light, Aster noticed a grim look of worry on her face. Professor Andromeda's jaw clenched, and her hand went to a chain around her neck. She let out a sigh of relief when Roark threw them a rope. Apparently, Aster wasn't the only one worried about the possibility of an ambush.

- 21 -

Chapter 3

Aster climbed up the rope, Andromeda following close behind. Roark hoisted them out of the hole without a word. He glanced around, then motioned for them to follow him into the woods. Suddenly, something whistled in Aster's ear.

"GET DOWN!" Roark yelled. "Andi, take Aster and hide in the woods. Now!"

Andromeda pulled Aster down as arrows continued to whistle over their heads. She grabbed her arm and pulled, crawling along the ground. Aster heard the twang of the arrows aimied straight at them.

Andromeda pulled her up, and they ran crouched the rest of the way until they passed the first line of trees. Aster felt the world spinning around her. In her shock, she felt like a fog surrounded her entire being.

"Aster, stay here! I'm going to help Roark!"

Andromeda dug out two bows and sets of arrows from a pile of leaves. In her mental fog, Aster realized they must have been planning for a quick exit for quite some time. Andromeda bolted out of the woods to help Roark, but Aster's legs seemed stuck to the ground.

She was no help, a lump on a log.

Aster could only heard the whistles of the arrows and thumps of the assailants Roark and Professor Andromeda successfully hit. A moment ago, they were standing in the clearing, relieved and hopeful, and now this. It felt impossible. Aster had never felt her heart beating so hard. Her breathing became raspy as panic shook her to the core. Her mental fog vanished almost immediately when hands suddenly grabbed her from behind and began dragging her backwards, away from Professor Andromeda and Roark.

Aster screamed when she finally found her voice. The muscles in her legs activated, and she began kicking her feet and digging her heels into the ground, trying to stop her attacker from pulling her farther into the woods. The attacker tried to lift her off the ground, but Aster fought with all her might.

"Aster, stop it!"

She recognized the voice immediately.

Josiah.

He used his strength and spun her around to face him. She stopped fighting him, and he grabbed onto her shoulders, holding her away from him.

"Aster, I'm here to help. I've been waiting here, as Roark instructed me."

She stopped struggling, and Josiah let her go cautiously.

He grabbed her arm again, and once again she fell on the ground hard, barely dodging an arrow that whistled above her head and found its mark in the tree behind Josiah.

"Aster, who attacked you all?" he asked, keeping them both flat on the ground.

"I don't know," Aster answered. "It all happened so quickly. We made it out of the tunnel from the school, and Roark saw nothing until they started firing. It's all a blur. Professor Andromeda pulled me down and dragged me in here, and then you scared me half to death."

"Sorry about that," he said with a harsh laugh. "I figured Roark told you I was out here keeping watch just in case."

"Well, you did a great job," Aster snapped, though she instantly regretted her words.

Josiah tensed beside her, and she twisted her head toward the shadows of Roark and Andromeda fighting off their attackers.

"Sorry," she said. "I shouldn't have said that. I'm sure you did your best."

Josiah stayed silent and tense, and Aster mentally berated herself for lashing out at him.

The fear and anxiety were wearing on her.

Out of nowhere, Professor Andromeda suddenly burst through the brush and into the woods, Roark following a second later. Aster got up, pulling away from Josiah.

"Aster, there you are!" Andi cried.

Roark pushed past them, heading straight for Josiah, who was getting up off the ground, his face going from red to white in an instant.

Roark grabbed the front of Josiah's shirt and slammed him against a tree. Aster protested, but Andi held her back, shaking her head.

"I told you to stay alert and watch the exit!"

Roark said with such quiet intensity that it frightened Aster, and she wasn't even the one in hot water.

"I told you, if I let you join this mission, you had to be focused. You couldn't let your guard down. You must stay vigilant. We almost died out there. They almost hit Aster! If Andi and I hadn't survived, how do you imagine you all would have made it to Topiarius?"

Josiah tried to answer, but Roark didn't give him a chance.

"I should make you stay here and fend for yourself. Eventually, they'll notice you're gone and do the math. If they find you, you know what will happen. I won't do that right now, but that doesn't mean I won't if you show such a lack of attention next time."

He released Josiah with such force he fell to the side, catching himself with one arm as he hit the ground. Josiah glanced back up at Roark with remorse, but remorse quickly turned to anger.

He pushed himself up level with Roark. "I did my job! I watched, and there was no sign of the enemy! Perhaps we wouldn't be running if you hadn't waited till the last minute to take Aster to the Academy! You knew she was the one, but you kept saying to wait, 'just so we're sure!' It's not my fault they attacked you! This whole thing could've been avoided if you hadn't been so scared!"

Roark stared at Josiah with ice-cold eyes. Aster almost wish he'd do something; his stillness and silence kept her on edge.

Andromeda stepped in and took charge, not wanting the situation to escalate any further.

"It doesn't matter what any of us did. We can only look forward to the task ahead. That task is to take Aster safely to the Academy. Our journey is doomed if you both don't let go of your anger."

Josiah hung his head, though his shoulders stayed tensed, and nodded. Roark also nodded brusquely and stalked off into the woods.

Andromeda sighed and shook her head. "Okay, you two, let's go."

Aster feared the tension would only continue to grow as they journeyed forward.

The woods became denser as they continued their journey. The trees created a shield above, to where they couldn't see even a speck of sky. No one said a word, though Aster had about a thousand racing through her mind.

"Are there many others who believe in the Legend?" Aster asked hesitantly.

Andromeda answered, "Yes, but we're becoming fewer and fewer. The Evanders have done well at hiding the truth."

"What about my parents, do they.-" Aster's breath caught in her throat. She stopped in her tracks.

Her family!

Josiah, not watching, came up behind her, almost knocking her down.

"Aster, come, on we can't stop," he grumbled.

"Aster, Josiah's right." Andromeda sighed, turning around to check on them. "We have to keep going. You can do this, let's go."

"No!" Aster finally got out, and at this, Roark finally stopped and whipped around.

Aster took a shallow breath, panic setting in. "What I mean is, what about my family? The Evanders probably know I'm with you, and if they know we're headed to this-Academy, what will keep them from going to my family and hurting them, or…"

She couldn't even finish her sentence, because the train of thought she was taking almost suffocated her.

She bent forward, feeling like someone punched her in the gut, the wind knocked out of her and head reeling.

Andromeda hurried over to her. "Aster, calm down. Look at me," she said, grabbing Aster's shoulders and pulling her up. "Aster, look at me. There, now listen, we sent word to your parents before we left. I made sure that they were taken care of, and Josiah escorted your brothers and sister home after he told Roark about the journal. They're already being taken to a safe house, then they'll travel to Toparius when the coast is clear."

Aster's breathing still felt shallow, she could just picture the fear in her sister's face and the worry this must be causing her mother. Andromeda rubbed Aster's shoulders, trying to soothe her, but it wasn't helping much. Roark didn't give any reassurances, but Aster felt Josiah's hand on her arm.

She looked at him, the question in her eyes.

"They were fine when I left them," Josiah said reassuringly. "Your sister was frightened at first, but then she started saying you must have done something really bad for them to get sent home and you to have to stay in the headmaster's office. Your brothers seemed to sense something might be wrong, but I tried playing it off."

Aster let out a hollow laugh and rolled her eyes. Of course, her sisters would say that.

"Your parents took the news in stride," he added in an odd tone. "They'll be fine, and you will see them again soon. They know where we're headed, and they'll come when it's safe."

Aster nodded, breathing a little deeper this time.

"That's if we keep moving and don't stay here talking." Roark said from ahead, already moving onward.

Andromeda scowled at his back, clearly not happy with his continued sour attitude, but she let it go and, after making sure Aster was behind her, followed him as they continued tramping through the woods.

Hours later, Aster could tell it was getting dark and felt relief when Roark stopped walking.

"We'll camp here tonight and continue first thing in the morning," he stated.

Josiah dropped his pack and reached inside, bringing out a couple of rolled blankets, handing them to Andromeda and Aster.

"I'm going to see what food I can find." He grabbed a knife from his bag and left without another word.

Aster watched him leave and could sense something was still wrong with him. She prided herself on being able to read people's emotions. Though her mother and father always told her to leave people be.

"No one wants you prying," her father would say.

She never saw it as prying, though. If she knew how they were feeling, she could help them easier. However, her parents never agreed with her logic on the matter.

"A penny for your thoughts?" Andromeda asked, sitting down beside her.

Aster laughed. "I have a lot more thoughts right now than a penny's worth." She sighed. "Can you tell me more about the Legend—sorry, the story of Ignis? As in the actual story? And how do the journal or I, fit into it? And what's a Light Keeper, exactly?" Aster rambled off her list of questions waiting to be answered.

Andromeda glanced over at Roark, who was poring over his maps, oblivious to anything else.

"Well, she began, when the King banished Gaia and Tarronand others still loyal to him, he gave them a book. Ironically, he entrusted it to Gaia and Tarron, but that's how much he cared for them, despite what they did," Andromeda added passionately. "The book contained myriad knowledge, from the proper history of Ignis to everything else they would need to teach the next generation of Light Keepers."

"But what are Light Keepers, exactly?" Aster repeated.

"Oh, right, I'm getting ahead of myself," Andi apologized. "When Ignis was whole, there were some born with special abilities, Light Keepers. Quarriers could control the earth,

Divums the sky, but Nimuses, the most unique Light Keepers, could control the mind. Gaia and Tarron had powers of sky and mind, but the King took their powers when he banished them. He said they had lost the wonderful privilege, but the powers would return to their children and their children's children."

Aster felt a thrill of excitement as Andromeda continued the story.

"The book was used to teach the next generations. As their family grew, they spread out across the three lands. Those who left Veridi created an Academy in Vela and Gemma. Gaia and Tarron stayed here to create the one in Veridi."

"Is it in Toparius? Is that why we're going there? But I never heard of these Academies. I've never read about them in my books," Aster interrupted.

"Because the Evanders have worked hard to find and destroy them," Roark commented from his spot, where he had been listening.

Andromeda sighed. "Yes, the Evanders became afraid of the Light Keepers and their goal to reunite Ignis. They preferred control. They tried to make the Legend a joke, and when that failed, they made it their goal to destroy the Academies, and anyone involved."

"And I'm supposed to help reunite Ignis?" Aster asked.

"It's every Light Keeper's purpose to work toward reuniting the lands," Andi stated, her voice rising passionately again. "But the King told Gaia and Tarron one day a group of three would find the Knight, and he will restore Ignis to its former glory. It's said the three will come from their family line."

"Professor Andromeda-"

"Please Aster, you can call me Andromeda or just Andi." Aster smiled and nodded. "Andi, if I'm a Light Keeper, what are my powers?" Aster had a million questions pressing on her mind, but this had been gnawing at her since Andi told her she was a Light Keeper.

Andi glanced quickly at Roark.

"Andi, don't," Roark snapped. "It's not the right time to tell her, we need to keep moving."

Andi sighed but nodded in reluctant agreement. But Aster didn't agree. She didn't agree at all.

"Tell me, please," Aster asked, a little more demanding than she meant to sound.

"Aster, we'll tell you, but not yet," Roark said. "It's late enough as it is, and you've had a lot thrown at you already. We'll eat, then we're going to rest. Trust me, you'll need it."

Then he left, leaving no room for argument or discussion. A short while later, Josiah returned with wild game, fixed a fire, and roasted the animal on a spit he'd made from a branch. Roark wanted them all to rest, but as Aster lay there in the dark, she couldn't imagine finding sleep. Everything about her life had changed in an instant.

They stuck to Roark's plan and woke up early the next day. The trees became less thick as they continued onward, and by late afternoon, they stepped out of the thick woods and entered a large clearing filled with sunlight. Aster's shoulders relaxed at the sight of a tiny cottage sitting beautifully in the middle of the clearing, the light shining down from the opening above, providing the cottage with its own spotlight. She felt safe here, though she couldn't put her finger on why.

"Ah, well, she's home," Andi said, nodding to the smoke curling gracefully from the stone chimney.

"She?" Aster asked.

"Yes," Andi said, "this is one of our safe houses. We've always been able to count on Mag to help us throughout the years. She didn't like what she saw the country becoming, especially with the Intrusions. She moved away from the towns and villages to this little spot. It's a benefit to us because it's situated perfectly, away from any unwanted attention. Especially since someone started the rumor that these parts are haunted," She added with a sly look at Josiah.

He shrugged. "What can I say? I'm good at making up stories."

Aster's head swiveled back and forth as she took in her surroundings. A small chicken coop stood over to the right, a garden beside it filled with a ripe harvest. To the left of the cottage stood a rustic, wooden barn with horses munching on hay in the corral outside. Aster distinctively heard a moo coming from a cow ready to be milked, and she smiled at the overall homey feeling of the clearing. What caught her eye, almost immediately, were the beautiful wildflowers surrounding the house and sprouted up its sides. Their vines trailed up from the ground, snaking their way up the chimney. They surrounded one window and spread out across the gabled roof. Their fragrance was intoxicating, and Aster took a deep breath filled with memories and thoughts of spring and summer back home. A pang of longing filled her.

She remembered the days, of taking walks with her family when she was younger, picking flowers, taking picnics on lazy summer days with the breezes blowing to cool them off. She wondered if she would ever see her family again, let alone her home. If she did, she would insist they take walks again.

Something had changed as she grew up. Her parents and siblings became exasperated with her, and her siblings found their own friends and hobbies to occupy their time. They left her alone to read and daydream; she didn't mind, but it hadn't helped her much with making friends. She wished she could pinpoint the moment the shift in their lives had happened, but her memory always became foggy and dark when she tried to reach too far back. It often bothered her she couldn't remember much of her past, but whenever the curiosity of it all became overwhelming or scary, she pushed it aside. She felt something there in her memories, something she had forgotten for a reason. She wasn't sure she wanted to reawaken whatever monster of the past lurked behind that curtain.

"Aster," Andi said, touching her arm.

Aster jumped and realized everyone was staring at her, concerned, all except one. A woman whom she hadn't noticed come out of the house. Her shoulders were bent with the weight of her years, and her white hair with streaks of gray was neatly pinned up in a braid on top of her head. The older woman looked curiously at Aster. A slight grin sat in the corner of her mouth, and Aster felt like the woman's eyes understood what she herself did not.

"I'm sorry," Aster said, trying to look away from the woman, "I wasn't paying attention."

"Aster," Andi said again, her eyes wide with concern, "you've not responded for almost five minutes. We were saying your name, calling out, but you just stood here."

Aster felt dazed. She had gotten lost that long in her clouds, so unaware. "I guess I just became…"

"Lost in thought," the older woman finished for her.

She hobbled over to Aster, who glanced at Andi and Roark, alarmed, but they looked as confused as she felt. The woman was shorter than Aster, but her presence made Aster feel like an ant, scared of the boot looming over it. The woman studied her face. Aster felt like she was reading from it all of her thoughts, her history, and maybe even her future.

"Aster," Andi said, breaking the silence, "this is Mag."

"It's nice to meet you," Aster said, almost in a whisper.

She stuck out her hand to shake Mag's, but the old woman just kept staring at her.

"Yes," Mag said, causing Aster to startle. "She has something there. Her mind needs strength. It needs training. You were right to take her away. She needs training and protection only the Academy can give her right now."

Aster felt mute. She had many questions, but they wouldn't come; her mouth felt glued shut. Mag nodded and walked back to the cottage with a new strength.

"Come in, all of you. We have much to discuss before you leave here. You'll stay the night and get rested in order to continue your journey."

Andi and Roark filed inside behind Mag, while Josiah stayed back with Aster.

"It's going to be okay, Aster," he encouraged.

"Are you sure about that?" she asked.

All he could give her was a shrug before following the others.

Aster stood outside the cottage. She closed her eyes and took a deep breath. The clearing smelled like so many memories from her childhood, the good and the bad. However, she worried the beauty outside wouldn't be as enjoyable after whatever she was about to learn on the inside.

Chapter 4

The cottage looked tiny on the outside, but Aster found it quite roomy inside. They entered a long hallway from the front door and followed Mag to the end of the hallway into a large kitchen. The kitchen was larger than Aster had imagined finding. She wondered if someone had purposefully created the outside to look smaller. She also wondered what else the cottage was hiding.

The kitchen contained a gigantic stone fireplace to their right, with a wide mouth to hold the black kettle hanging inside. A fire crackled underneath the kettle, with a comforting aroma wafting from its depths. On the wall facing them was a large table with herbs, other ingredients, and various-size pestles strewn about in a deliberate fashion. Dried flowers hung from the ceiling surrounded by pots and pans, a fresh loaf of bread sat on the table, and a cat laid on the hearth, not caring enough to give the visitors a second glance. Aster felt a sense of familiarity with the room, with Mag.

Mag seemed to sense her feelings. "There will be time to answer your questions later, Aster. Let us first sit and eat, then you'll tell me what brought you all here."

They sat at the long, sturdy table in the middle of the kitchen as Mag handed them plates and passed around the bread, along with a plate of cheese and meats she seemed to produce out of thin air. They remained quiet as they ate, realizing just how hungry they were after walking so far. Aster had to remind herself to chew before swallowing. She didn't want to seem as if she lacked manners, but the hunger won out over decorum. They remained in silence, collecting their thoughts, until Mag spoke up again, this time addressing Roark.

"Now, Roark, explain what led you to take the girl away so suddenly."

Aster thought by the sound of that question it seemed Mag had already known about her before today, which sent a chill down her spine.

Roark cleared his throat. "Yesterday morning, Josiah came to me and reported that Aster told him about a journal she found in her family library. She wasn't able to make out all the words, but she caught one—the name Intruder."

Mag's shoulders stiffened at the name as it left Roark's lips, but she stayed silent, allowing him to continue.

Roark explained how he and Andi had told Aster as much as they could, and of course, about their attackers.

"I'm not sure who attacked us, though I have a good guess it was the Evanders. We made it through the tunnels, but they ambushed us a moment later."

He looked at Josiah, but a nudge from Andi caused him to stop before placing blame again. Mag ignored the interaction and motioned for him to continue.

"We took care of them and headed straight here. The original plan was to travel straight to the Academy, but we couldn't make it, considering the circumstances. The Evanders coming to the school changed everything. It's possible we could have made it out of the city at night. But they took us by surprise. I couldn't risk them following us to the river. I knew we'd have to take the path through the forest instead."

Mag stared at her hands as he spoke, nodding now and then, but stayed silent even after he finished. No one said a word. Aster could hear the cat purring by the fireplace. The room was so quiet. Eventually, Mag looked up and put her withered hand on Roark's shoulder.

"You did the right thing. It wasn't the original plan, but we've all learned to switch gears in this life of ours. We do not set our plans in stone. Now, child," she said, looking to Aster, who shrank back under her gaze. "Tell me about this journal. I suppose you all brought it with you in your quick escape?"

Andi produced the journal from her satchel and handed it to Mag, who gingerly took the faded red leather and peered at it with great concentration. A smile crept from her mouth, and she nodded at the journal in her hand, as if it had spoken to her.

"Yes, I hoped it might be this one. I haven't seen it for decades."

"What's special about it, though?" Aster asked. "I know Andi said they instructed every Light Keeper to keep one, but what's so special about this one specifically?"

Aster desperately hoped Mag would eventually explain what the missing part of the legend said about her.

"You all haven't told her?" Mag asked. She didn't sound angry, but Aster could sense the disappointment.

Sighing, she opened the journal and pointed Aster to the inside cover.

"You see this symbol?" Mag asked quietly.

Aster nodded; it was the symbol of fire.

"This isn't just any Light Keeper's journal. This journal belonged to the line of the Guardians, Gaia and Tarron. And according to the Legend, their children will find the Knight and reunite Ignis. That's why they believe you're one of the three."

Mag pointed a withered finger at the name etched on the back of the journal in gold leaf, *Hestia Tarron – Nimus.*

Aster gasped, recognizing the name.

"Yes." Mag nodded. "This journal belonged to your great-grandmother. Which means you come from the line of Gaia and Tarron."

Aster knew her mouth was hanging open, but she couldn't find it in her to close it.

The realizations fell heavily on her shoulders.

She realized why Andi and Roark had watched her.

Everything that made her different seemed to make sense now.

Mag glanced down, and Aster knew she was avoiding looking at her. Aster felt everyone knew something she didn't.

SNAP. They all jumped at the sound of Mag closing the book and letting it fall on the table. She seemed ready to talk about what she read, and they all leaned in, ready to listen, but to their disappointment, she got up and went over to the large black kettle over the fireplace to stir whatever concoction she had brewing.

"You can't leave this to settle," she remarked. "Give it attention. If you don't, if you forget about it, it will settle to the bottom and burn,becoming useless to the needs of those who are hungry for it."

Aster felt the heavy silence, as they all listened to the old lady's musings. The only sound was the crackling fire.

"Aster, hand me the black bottle behind you on the top shelf, and the red bottle on the bottom shelf," Mag instructed.

Aster glanced at Andi and Roark for an explanation, but they prodded her to do as Mag instructed. She rose, her chair scraping the floor and filling the quiet kitchen with noise. Aster grabbed the bottles gently off the top and bottom shelf full of different herbs, spices, a container for sugar, and one for flour. She held the glass bottles carefully, just imagining herself dropping them and the beautiful glass shattering, sending shards flying everywhere. But she held her grip, despite her nervously shaking, sweaty hands, and held them out to Mag.

"Open the black one first," Mag said. "But smell it before pouring it in," she added with an almost mischievous grin.

Aster gingerly brought it up to her nose and smelled it; couldn't keep herself from turning her head to gag at the bitter smell coming from inside the dark bottle, like every foul smell in the world had been mixed together. Aster couldn't believe Mag was about to add it to the food she was fixing, and she didn't want to eat whatever came out of the bubbling mixture inside the kettle. Mag laughed at Aster's reaction and took the bottle from her.

She allowed three or more drops to plop down into the kettle and a puff of black smoke unfurled from inside, sending the acrid smell through the once-cozy kitchen. The others coughed as the smell hit them, and Andi covered her mouth and nose against it. Mag looked at them all and shook her finger at Andi.

"No, now don't cover your nose from the smell. If you can't handle the bitter, you won't be able to handle the sweet," she reprimanded.

Andi lowered her hand, her face flushing.

"Now," Mag said, turning her eyes back to the kettle, "hand me the red bottle, but smell it first."

Aster was afraid of what smell would meet her nose this time, but she did as Mag instructed. She quickly lifted the red bottle to her nose, expecting another horrible smell to singe it. However, the smell of cherries—or, no, strawberries or something sweet—greeted her instead. Aster couldn't put a name to the smell, but it made her smile. Her heart felt lighter and full of hope.

Mag added the same three-to-six drops into the kettle. Instead of black smoke, a red vapor issued up from the pot into the kitchen, swirling around the room and filling it with a wonderful smell. The others' faces told Aster they, too, were experiencing the same feeling.

"It smells like cinnamon," Josiah said.

"No, no," Roark said. "It smells like roses, sweet roses in the morning dew." He glanced at Andi and smiled.

"You're both wrong," Andi said with a smile for Roark. "It smells like honeysuckle, fresh honeysuckle at the first of spring."

Mag looked at Aster. "Aster, what did you smell?"

"I smelled cherries or strawberries, something sweet."

"Wait," Roark said. "Mag, how can we all smell something different? It's not possible."

"Tsk, tsk." Mag peered back into the pot.

"It's not the smell that matters," Aster said without thinking.

Mag didn't reply. She just kept stirring, the black and red mixing into a beautiful maroon that almost seemed to sparkle. The others looked at Aster, and she realized they were waiting for her to finish explaining.

Her cheeks reddened at their attention: she was not used to people wanting to hear what she had to say.

"We all smelled something different but had the same feeling. I could tell on all of your faces, you felt it."

"Name it," Mag said without looking up.

"Hope," Aster said, staring at Mag with great curiosity and less trepidation. "We all felt hope."

The others looked at each other in surprise, confirming Aster's theory. They smiled, and the tension in the room dissipated with the red vapor as it swirled out of the kitchen window.

"Aster," Mag said, breaking the spell, "taste this." She held up the spoon from the pot, with the odd-colored mixture steaming off it.

Aster was a little hesitant, but she chose to trust Mag. She took the spoon, closed her eyes, put the hot liquid on her mouth, and swallowed. The liquid fell down her throat and tasted unlike anything she had ever tasted before or would ever taste again. The flavors danced on tongue, moving from savory bitters to sweet and tangy.

Its warmth lifted her spirits even more than the smell. "It's incredible," was all she could say.

Mag covered the pot, allowing the liquid to simmer. "Something you must know before I explain the journal," she said. "You must agree to what I say before we go any further."

Without hesitating, Aster nodded.

"In life, you'll experience good and bad. Accepting both is key. No matter what happens next, no matter what you learn in the coming days and when you reach the Academy, you must accept the bad along with the good. Just like this pot, if you fail to stir it up, to mix in the bitter herbs and the sweet tangs, it won't taste as intended. Without the bad things, we can't completely appreciate the good when it comes."

Aster wondered at Mag's analogy. What bad things would she soon learn?

Mag ambled back to the table and sat down.

"Your great-grandmother, like other Light Keepers, was given a journal, but as a Nimus, her journal contains more in it than others might have."

"What can Nimuses do? Andi said they control the mind, but how is that possible?"

Mag gave Andi and Roark another mild look of disappointment.

"Roark believed it would be better to tell her this part here," Andi said in defense, though clearly not in agreement with his decision.

"Tell me what?" Aster asked.

Mag sighed. "In Ignis, before the earthquake, it was common for people to be born with certain abilities—"

"—Mind, sky, and earth," Aster finished.

Mag nodded. "Each generation following the earthquake produced a handful of children with one of these three abilities, though they have become fewer and fewer. They became feared by the Evanders, so many parents began hiding their children or tried damping their powers altogether. However, there were still those who believed and fostered their children's gifts by sending them to the safety of the Academy."

Mag paused, and Aster began putting the pieces together.

"My great-grandmother was a Nimus—and that means I might be one as well…" Aster stated.

"Not might," Mag corrected. "There's no doubt you are a Nimus, and a quite a powerful one I imagine, with your lineage. The moment you came into the clearing and became lost in your thoughts, I knew it."

Aster felt a buzzing inside her head. Her heartbeat inside her chest. She felt a sense of relief. Growing up, everyone had made her feel like something was wrong with her. This knowledge of her heritage, though, gave her oddities a whole new meaning.

Mag gazed at her as she processed this knowledge.

"What does this mean, exactly?" Aster asked breathlessly.

"Light Keepers need much training to use their ability. Much of it you already do without realizing; think about it."

"My daydreaming," Aster stated.

"Yes, daydreaming is part of it. That's searching your mind, creating stories, your own world. However, a time will come when you'll be able to search the minds of others. I'd venture to say you're already quite good at reading people."

Aster caught Josiah smirking. "Sometimes annoyingly so," he said with a friendly grin.

Aster glared at him, then turned back to Mag.

"This is a lot to take in," she said to no one in particular.

Andi reached out across the table and patted her hand. "It's going to be okay, Aster. We'll help you as much as we can."

Aster smiled.

"Aster," Roark whispered, "I'm sorry we didn't tell you sooner."

They all looked at him, confused.

Roark sighed. "I felt the suspicions pointed toward Andi and me for a few months now, but I kept ignoring them. Neither one of us was sure of Aster's abilities. I didn't want to rush until I felt sure. But I believe someone either overheard Aster telling Josiah about the journal or Josiah telling me about what Aster said. Either way, my hesitancy almost cost us everything."

Andi put her hand on Roark's arm. "It's not your fault," she said. "We don't know how long they knew about us. They might not even know about the journal. Maybe they just randomly chose today."

Roark didn't reply, and Aster felt bad for him taking on such guilt.

Mag shook her head. "Stop throwing blame around," she said, looking at each of them. "Nothing could change what happened today. Everything happens when it is supposed to and not a second later. We need to put our energy into preparing you all for the next leg of your journey instead of taking on guilt."

The chair scraped across the floor again as she stood up from the table, making her point it was time to move on and focus on the task ahead.

"Now," she said, "Josiah, prepare the horses. Andi, fill the bags I've set out for you with whatever you need from the kitchen and gardens. I already prepared a medical bag that you can take with you as well."

Andi and Josiah went off to their tasks, and Mag turned her attention to Roark. "Look on my desk and you'll find the maps you need. Take the letters there as well. I need them to go to the Academy with you."

Aster stood there as Roark left her and Mag alone, and she wondered what task she could do to help, since they were in this because of her.

Mag turned to her and handed her the journal. "Aster, you're going to come with me. I want us to look at this journal together."

Chapter 5

Aster followed Mag outside to the garden.

"You knew my great-grandmother?" she asked as they walked past fragrant blossoms of jasmine.

"Yes, I did. I met her when I was a young girl at the Academy," Mag said, smiling at the reminiscence.

"You went to the Academy?" Aster asked, surprised. "That means you're a Light Keeper, too?"

Aster wanted to ask what ability Mag possessed, but she kept that thought to herself, not knowing how polite it was to ask such a question.

Mag smiled mischievously. "I think you already know the answer to that."

Aster gasped; Mag had read her thoughts—that was the only way she could have known.

"A Nimus," Aster replied.

Mag just smiled and kept walking through her garden. Aster held back and looked at the garden in its entirety.

"Your garden is beautiful," she commented.

It wasn't a large garden. Despite its smaller size, though, Aster felt like she could get lost in all the beautiful foliage and flowers that surrounded her. Her mother had taught her a lot about flowers and how to take care of them. It was one time when Aster's curiosity had been helpful. She'd learned which flowers needed sun, and which ones wanted more shade. The ones who loved the sun her mother would surround the front with, but the shade lovers filled out the back of their house, and under the trees where Aster and her siblings liked to play and read. A memory swiftly enveloped Aster like a soft cloud.

One day when they'd all been outside, her mother tending to the flowers, Amity had raced to the swing their father had tied to a sturdy tree branch, and she'd called out for Aster to come push her. Aster remembered skipping past her mother, skimming her hand over the soft petals of the flowers, and joining her sister at the swing. With a great shove, she'd pushed her back and forth, becoming distracted when her brothers raced around them, seeing who could run the fastest. Then Amity had cried for Aster to push her higher and higher. Aster had laughed and pushed with all her might, imagining her sister flying like a little bird, off into the clouds and above the house. Aster remembered wishing she could fly like a bird as well, when she fell backward and blacked out. The next thing she remembered was waking up on the ground, her mother hovering over her, Amity crying out that it wasn't her fault, and the brothers shaking their heads, saying something that sounded a lot like, "She's so weird."

Aster felt cold, a shiver going up her spine.

"What's wrong?" Mag asked, peering at her.

"Nothing," Aster lied.

Mag gave her a shrewd look, and Aster knew she wasn't fooling her at all.

"I had a memory—something I hadn't thought about for years. I'm not even sure it happened."

Mag shrugged. "That happens to many of us."

Aster shook her head. "This is different, though. Whenever a memory surfaces, I feel like I'm not seeing the full picture."

She had never voiced these feelings. But she had been experiencing this memory loss for a while. She was always afraid her parents wouldn't understand. However, she felt of all people, Mag would understand her, or at least try to understand.

Mag motioned to her. "Sit, and maybe we can make things a little clearer."

"You can help me regain my memory?" Aster asked, sitting down on the garden bench beside Mag's slight frame.

"No, I can't help you with your memory. Regaining your memories will come with time and through your own power. But don't worry," Mag added, seeing Aster's disappointment. "It will come—whether you still want it afterwards is a different matter."

Before Aster could ask what she meant, Mag pointed a bony finger at the journal.

"Let's open it, shall we?" she said with a grim smile.

Aster opened the journal hesitantly, feeling like it weighed a ton with the mysteries it held inside for her. She leafed through the pages and came upon a pair that were stuck together, whether purposely or through the wear and tear of being passed around by her family. She separated them, worried that she might rip both, but she could feel something between them. The pages came apart, and a piece of paper fluttered out from between them, falling smoothly to the ground. Aster glanced at Mag but couldn't tell if she seemed startled or not. Had she known someone wedged this between these pages?

"Well, pick it up, girl," Mag said.

Aster did as she was told and unfolded the piece of paper. It was a letter in an unfamiliar script. However, she noticed a note from her great-grandmother scrawled in the top right corner.

It read:

I found this among the papers saved from one of the recent storms in Vela. The storm severely damaged the Academy and their archives there. Thankfully, this letter was in my possession at the time, and I've done my best to keep it safe. I'm going to keep it hidden, though, until I can decipher its true meaning. This could change everything. This could lead us closer to finding the way to the Knight and ultimately to reunite Ignis.

Aster's heart began beating fast, her eyes rapidly scanning the letter's contents,

My King,

I have found the way to defeat the darkness, but I fear it will overcome me before my search can begin. Even now, I hear the heavy feet of darkness coming for me. In case they intercept this message, I leave this knowledge with you, hoping someone will bring these elements together and help light my way back to save our kingdom.

For the Darkness to Unbind,
You must find
The Flower with a Royal Mind.
A Star Combined
And a Jewel unmined
Together These Three
Will lead the way for Thee.

Aster felt a mixture of excitement and dread fill her.

"Well?" Mag asked, catching Aster before she became lost in her thoughts. "What is it?"

"It's a letter," Aster said. "I believe it's from the Knight himself, written to the King. Something about him defeating the darkness. It must be the ones you said, the only ones who can find the Knight are three heirs of Gaia and Tarron. He wrote it as a poem, so it's not straight forward. I suppose he did that in case the Intruder intercepted the letter."

Mag shook her head. "You're almost right."

Aster looked at her, confused. "What do you mean? That's what it says right here. What part did I misunderstand?" She prided herself on being able to discern things correctly.

"We've already identified one heir, leaving only two more to find," Mag said matter-of-factly.

Aster's stomach dropped as if she had fallen from a significant height, and she had to remind herself to breathe. She didn't want to continue in the direction of this conversation. She had a sinking suspicion about what Mag was about to say next.

"No," Aster said, standing up and pacing in front of the bench. "No," she repeated. "First, you tell me I have a mystical ability, and now you're saying not only do I have this power, but I'm going to help find the long-lost Knight and help reunite a country split into thirds by a mystical earthquake?"

It couldn't be.

It made little sense. Yet, it did.

Her mother had always told her they named her after the asters growing near their house, but what if it there was more to her name?

My thoughts, my daydreams, what if they're something more?

"Impossible!" she said, stopping the trail her thoughts were about to take.

She would not have Mag force her into a role not meant for her. Mag and the others needed to find the Knight, and perhaps in their desperation, they believed she was one of the three keys.

Aster wasn't even sure she believed the Legend to be true. The information was quite a lot to handle all at once. The weight of it lay heavily on her shoulders, and she stopped pacing and slumped back down on the bench, feeling exhausted.

"It's not impossible," Mag said. "You are '*The Flower with a Royal Mind,*' Aster. You can try to deny it all you want, but I knew it the moment I saw you, and I know you can sense it, too."

Mag smiled and nodded.

Aster laughed in disbelief.

"Consider it," Mag pushed. "You'll see I'm right. Your mind is something special, and your ability is something unique, and powerful."

Aster didn't want to consider anything.

"There are other Nimuses, right?" Aster asked, grasping at straws."

"Yes, but you are an heir to Gaia and Tarron. The Light Keeper emblem inside the journal leaves no doubt—you are '*The Flower with a Royal Mind.*'"

She couldn't reflect about it too much, or she felt she'd end up agreeing with Mag, and that would change everything. She put her head in her hands. What was she thinking? Everything had already changed. The moment she picked up that journal, she could feel it. She felt it again when they entered the clearing and, in the kitchen, standing by the fire with Mag.

How can reading minds help find the Knight? Aster thought to herself.

Mag answered her thoughts, "That's something you're going to find out—soon. You daydream, and sometimes so intensely that you become wholly unaware of what is going on around you. You're not exactly present. You've floated away in the clouds, so to speak. No matter how loud someone calls out to you, you can't hear them. In your daydreaming, you create stories, you think about things you have seen, heard, or learned. Your daydreams have more potential for power than you realize.

"Your parents have worried about it. They've tried to encourage you to stay in the present, to stay focused. Your teachers have done the same. Your daydreaming has cost you many friends because they don't understand you or your imagination. They don't understand you, so they fear you, and they exile you to the outskirts of their little groups."

Tears brimmed in Aster's eyes as Mag made her relive every horrible and sad memory from the past. Her family and friends had never truly understood or accepted her. Something inside her told her they hadn't always treated her like that, but when she tried to dig into her memories, she always found herself against a brick wall.

Mag sighed. "Don't struggle to see too far back, Aster. You're not ready for that yet. But don't worry, you will be, one day. Maybe sooner rather than later, but only you can decide that."

Aster looked at her with shock and disbelief still etched across her face. "But Mag, it can't be me. I'm… I'm me. I don't have a clue of the Knight's location. Until a few minutes ago, I thought he was a legend."

Mag smiled down at her, lifting her chin with her hand. "Aster, close your eyes."

Aster sighed but complied, closing her eyes.

"Now," Mag began, "when you first entered the clearing, it reminded you of something. You could see the memory, couldn't you?"

Aster nodded.

"Okay," Mag continued. "It happened in the kitchen as well. I could see it happen before my eyes. They may be old, but they still distinctly see the truth. Do you accept these moments happened?"

Aster nodded again.

"Accepting that these things happened is a step in the right direction," Mag said, releasing Aster's chin. "Keep your eyes closed, and I want you to take a deep breathe. Smell the surrounding flowers, feel the grass beneath you. Do you hear the tree limbs as they creak in the wind? Do you hear the horses whinny as Josiah saddles them for your journey? Take in the surrounding nature; let the peace fill you and calm you."

Aster took a deep breath, smelling the roses beside her, the lilacs behind her, and the sweet grass all around her in the calm and peaceful garden. She thought back to the kitchen, the intoxicating smell of Mag's concoction. The same feeling of hope and light she'd felt earlier swelled inside her.

"Now," Mag instructed, "feel the letter, picture the words, imagine the Knight as he wrote it…"

Mag's voice faded away, and Aster felt the letter burn against her palm, like a brand on an animal's hide. She couldn't let go. It felt sealed with glue on her hand. Aster could sense the writer's hurry as they penned the letter, the Knight's concern for his kingdom, his king, and all the people whose safety relied on him getting this letter out in time. Aster saw the Knight as clearly as if she were viewing a painting.

He sat with his back against a tree, hiding from the darkness, edging closer and closer. Even in her daydream, she could feel the weight of the darkness as it pressed in tighter. It thudded like the sound of hundreds of horses bearing down on a battlefield.

She saw the Knight finish his letter, roll it up, and send it away on his last carrier pigeon. The bird flew high above them, breaking through the trees and soaring into the clouds, flying fast for the kingdom. When Aster glanced back at the Knight, he was looking at her, and her breath caught. He could see her. Somehow, she knew he saw her as clearly as she saw him. The darkness drew closer. The Knight smiled instead of cowering.

"It's okay, this has to happen," he was telling her.

Run, *Aster thought desperately, but the Knight shook his head.*

The darkness slithered up behind him, and Aster's eyes widened in horror as the mass of darkness took form. Her dream became hazy before she could thoroughly see it. The Knight lifted his arm and held out his palm as if to push her away, but not before whispering, "Aster, go."

As quickly as the dream, or vision had occurred, it disappeared. Aster's eyes shot open. She gasped, falling back onto the grass, her chest heaving, sweat dripping down her forehead and neck. Yet, a strange peace also filled her. She pictured the Knight's face but couldn't recall details. She could only remember the peace she'd felt when his eyes were on her. He gave her a sense of hope that filled her with a confidence she had never felt before. She looked up at Mag, but the woman had moved. Aster sought around for her and saw her retreating form as it entered back into the cottage.

Aster sat there alone, trying to take in everything that had happened. She didn't understand how, but she had witnessed the moment the Knight wrote the letter, and he'd seen her. Was that mind searching? She realized she would discover the truth only if she went to the Academy. If she followed this path that was being laid out before her. The thought both thrilled and scared her.

She felt rooted to the ground, paralyzed by all the unknowns. She could hear the Knight telling her, Go. She got up, dusted herself off, and gathered her emotions, taking another step forward to the cottage. She didn't know what would transpire, what lay ahead of her, but she knew she'd have none of her answers if she didn't take the first step.

She found the others waiting for her in the kitchen, while Mag stood by the fire stirring the pot. Roark sealed up his maps and stuck the letters in his jacket pocket. Andi added the last of their provisions and was handing the bags to Josiah to strap to the horses he had readied. Questions filled their eyes.

Roark broke the silence. "Well, I think we're all ready. We'll stay here, since night will fall soon. First thing before dawn we'll ride out and head straight for the Academy."

Andi looked at Aster. "Are you ready, Aster?" she asked gently.

Aster surveyed their little group and looked down at the journal in her hand.

Was she ready?

Was she ready for what lay ahead?

Was she ready to discover her place in this legend made real?

Whether she was ready was hard to answer.

She gave the only answer she could, though: "I'm ready to go."

Out of the corner of her eye, she detected Mag smiling at her with a glint of pride in her eyes. But deep down, Aster didn't fully believe she was this Flower in the poem.

Whether she fully believed it yet didn't matter.

She had to follow the Knight's command.

"Go."

Chapter 6

Aster couldn't sleep. She tried reading from a book Roark had brought from his library. It only helped to excite her mind, thoughts bouncing all around it. The book explained what had happened after the Knight disappeared.

"A faction of the kingdom tried to take the Knight's place, to become part of the King's inner circle. It is said one of them, their leader, had a deep desire to one day dethrone the King and rule in his place. The rest of the kingdom opposed the idea and this faction of people. However, their audacity grew obnoxious and dangerous. To the point that the faction's leader stormed into the main square, trying to defame the King and move the people to his side. He believed he could be a better king or should have the chance to show that he could. He didn't think it was fair. The King only allowed the Knight to be advise him, to be rule by his side. The King didn't tolerate this kind of behavior in his kingdom. He was a loving king, but he was the King, and his wrath was as powerful as his mercy. He gave the leader and his group of anarchists the chance to stop what they were doing, and he would let them continue living in the kingdom. Witnesses say the group almost took him up on his offer, but their leader wouldn't hear of it, and he charged toward the King instead. The King's guards protected him, and the King banished the faction and their leader from the kingdom. He didn't do so happily, though; they say the King was quieter than usual and more withdrawn during the days following the banishment. He loved his people, but the way the faction had grown and the unrest they stirred up saddened him greatly."

No matter how hard she tried turning off her mind, sleep eluded her. Even despite the soothing sounds of nature, which would usually lull her to bed back home, she couldn't seem to shut off her thoughts, and it scared her. Plus, every time she tried to close her eyes, she saw the Knight, his deep-blue eyes staring at her, and the dark shadow taking form behind him. She knew she had to be careful after Mag's warning that she could literally become lost in her thoughts since she hadn't been trained how to control them yet. She didn't quite understand that, because in the past, she had always brought herself back, but she had to admit it was becoming harder and harder to pull herself out of the endless abyss. She looked over to where Andi slept peacefully and envied her. They would all need their sleep to be focused on the road ahead, both the physical and mental. Aster sighed and turned over, squeezing her eyes shut, but it didn't help. She thought about the peace she'd felt in the garden, and decided she would go out and walk around, and maybe that would help tire her out.

She walked carefully out of the room, praying the floor boards wouldn't creak under her footsteps. Once she made it to the kitchen, she grabbed a lantern from a shelf, lit it carefully, and stepped outside into the cool night air.

She meandered through the sleeping garden. The lantern helped her keep from stumbling, but the moon light from above gave her plenty of light without it.

Maybe this isn't a good idea, she suddenly thought to herself. But she was already outside and decided it couldn't hurt to keep walking around and enjoying the nighttime garden.

From her right, she heard a rustling in the bush near the forest, towards the back of the garden. Her mind imagined all sorts of different possibilities, and none of them were good. The rustling became louder, and she began backing away slowly, not wanting to put her back to whatever might come out of the woods. She held her breath, filled with fear, causing her to be unable to move.

A figure stepped out of the woods, and she almost screamed for help, but as it stepped closer into the moonlight, she realized it was Josiah.

"Aster?" he whispered incredulously into the darkness.

Her heart rate began to return to normal, but she felt her body still shaking from the fright he had given her.

"Josiah, what are you doing out in the woods?" she asked breathlessly.

"What are you doing out here in the garden in the middle of the night?" he volleyed back to her.

She crossed her arms defensively. "I couldn't sleep."

He laughed and nodded. "I'm keeping watch, but mainly because I couldn't sleep, either. Aster, this isn't a good idea for you. You never know who might've been out here. I haven't been able to tell how close any attackers from the school might be to us."

"I'm sorry, I'm not used to being hunted," she added with a harsh laugh. She crossed her arms against the cool evening breeze, wishing she had brought a coat. She felt vulnerable, out here, alone with Josiah.

He noticed her chill and gallantly took off his coat and put it across her shoulders. She bristled, not usually liking to be treated like a daisy, but it was chilly out here, and his coat was warm and eased the tension from her shoulders.

"Thank you," she said sincerely, pulling the coat closer around her.

Josiah smirked. "It's okay. I can understand it must be hard to sleep. You've had a big day today. They threw a lot of information at you at once, and anyone else would be buckling under the weight of it all. But you seem to be handling it well."

She looked at him with surprise. "I'm glad it looks like that. Let's just hope I can keep the façade going when we get to the Academy. I don't exactly fit the picture of heroine. I'm sure the moment they get a look at me, their hope at finding one of the three will be dashed to pieces."

Josiah looked at her intently. "Aster, the minute they meet you, they won't be able to doubt that you are the Flower with a Royal Mind."

Aster looked at him, wondering if the level of her shock registered in the dark. "How do you know? How do any of you know for sure?"

Josiah shrugged. "It makes sense. Mag obviously sensed something in you the moment she saw you come into the clearing. You're also the first one Roark and Andi have both agreed on. Plus, you daydream a lot, and you're just different. You don't fit in with any crowd, and even your siblings treat you differently."

"Wow," she said, feeling hurt and yet seen for the first time.

"Thanks for that wonderful observation of my lonely, outcast life." She turned to go, tired of this conversation now, but something he said finally registered with her. "Wait, you said that I'm the first one Roark and Andi have agreed on—what did you mean by that?"

Josiah suddenly didn't seem like he wanted to keep talking. "Me and my big mouth," he muttered, shaking his head.

"Josiah?" Aster pushed.

"They were just a couple who the Academy sent out to find descendants of Gaia and Tarron. Every time they thought they were on the right trail, it became obviously clear they weren't. They stopped in Verd on one of their journeys and saw you with your parents and siblings in the market. Something about you caught their eye, and they stayed until they felt sure they were on the right track with you."

"I don't remember seeing them before they started working at the school!" Aster said.

"They're very good at blending in and watching silently. You were still relatively young, though, for them to be completely sure, so they settled in and kept an eye on you the best way they knew how. Then they sent for me a year after they settled."

"Where were you?" Aster asked curiously, realizing for the first time she didn't know much about Josiah's life before he arrived in Verd.

"I was living at the Academy," Josiah said quietly.

"You lived at the Academy?!"

"I grew up there, really." He paused, and Aster could sense his feelings: a mix of happiness, pain, and loneliness.

He sighed and sat down in the middle of the garden where they stood. Aster sat down beside him, looking at him to finish his story.

"My parents were both Light Keepers. Despite them both having powers, I was born without. They traveled to the Academy often, and I was used to being surrounded by Light Keepers. I never understood why others feared them. But they did, and the more the Evanders came to fear them, the more they worked to silence them, or worse, eradicate them."

Aster had an awful feeling she knew where this story was headed.

"My parents had to go help a group of Light Keepers affected by one of the storms. They left me at the Academy to keep me safe… The message they received about the Light Keepers in danger was a trap.

"My parents wouldn't comply with being silent about the true history of Ignis, nor would they denounce their powers."

"Oh, Josiah, I'm so sorry." Aster put her hand on his arm; her heart ached for him.

"Word reached the Academy on what happened. Thankfully, they let me stay. Soon, I wasn't the only orphaned child of Light Keepers. From then on, though, I decided I would make it my mission to keep other Light Keepers safe."

"That's how you met Roark and Andi?" Aster asked.

"Yes. Roark had been at the Academy when my parents… when I started living there permanently. He took me under his wings after that. Andi came a few years later from Vela, though I'm not exactly sure what led her to come. Either way, she became like a mother to me, so obviously she and Roark became close. They became my family," Josiah said, smiling, remembering easier times.

"When they left on their mission," he continued, "I made them promise to let me help them. He said he would when he became settled. While I waited for them, I took what few missions I could to be more prepared for when I joined them."

Aster just looked up at the sky above, twinkling with stars. She had always seen Josiah as a friend, but never had she so highly respected him.

"Thank you, Josiah."

"For what?" he asked, confused.

"For choosing to make your tragedy mean something. For being my friend when no one else wanted to be."

"Aster, your differences make you who you are. It's good that you're not like everyone else back home. I recognized what your daydreaming was after living at the Academy so long surrounded by Light Keepers. Besides, everyone else back in Verd were boring and unimaginative. They make me fear for the future generations. If that's who's going to be the next leaders and inventors of our time, then we're in big trouble."

Aster tried not to laugh. She had always thought the same thing, but felt like she was the weird one and everyone else acted like a person should behave. Josiah had known what she was and accepted her. That meant more than he would ever know.

Instinctively, she reached over and grabbed his hand.

Aster looked over at him and saw that he was as surprised as she was. She quickly withdrew her hand and stood up.

"I should go and try to sleep; I think I'm finally getting tired," she said, turning back to the house. Then she realized she still had Josiah's coat. She began to shrug it off, but her stopped her.

"No, keep it tonight," he said. "An extra weight might help you fall asleep. At least, that's helped me in the past. I usually sleep with a bunch of quilts on top of me, even in the summer."

Aster smiled and pulled the coat back around her shoulders.

"Thanks," she said, and quickly walked back around the cottage, silently opened the back door, and went back into the house. She leaned against the door, a little breathless from the chilly air, and from something else she didn't want to admit.

Aster woke to the smell of something tantalizing coming from the kitchen. The sky had lightened, but it was still quite dark outside. She realized she must have finally drifted off to sleep some time ago, yet she could tell she didn't get near enough and still felt the tiredness weighing heavy on her. Josiah's coat was also weighing on her, and she shrugged it off, not wanting to elicit any questions from the others on why she had it in the first place. Aster noticed clothes laid out for her, no doubt by Andi, and she happily changed out of her school dress, which now looked stained and tattered beyond repair. After she changed into the pants and skirt Andi had left for her, she hung Josiah's coat back on one of the pegs near the front door, then made her way into the kitchen, her stomach growling at the smell of breakfast wafting through the cozy cottage. Andi and Josiah were in the kitchen already.

Andi was helping Mag fix breakfast, and Josiah was drinking coffee while looking over the maps Roark had gathered for their journey. He looked up when she came in, giving her a slight smile, which she returned.

"Good morning, Aster," Andi said, setting a platter of eggs on the table. "I hope you slept well. Roark wants us to be on our way as soon as possible, but I told him we couldn't expect to make it far on empty stomachs. We won't want to make a lot of stops, so we'll need to make sure we're fortified ahead of time."

Aster was thankful for Andi's thoughtfulness; she knew the others could probably make it fine, but this was all new to her. She could feel not only the physical but mental toll it was already taking on her.

"How can I help?" Aster asked, wanting to lend a hand and not feel like such a burden on them.

"You can take the toast off the stove top and put it on a plate. I think it should be done," Andi instructed, turning her attention back to the bacon Mag was fixing.

Aster took the toast off the stove top, careful not to burn her fingers. The warm bread felt good against the slight chill in the large kitchen. She piled the toast on a plate and set it by the eggs. She glanced at the map Josiah had laid out before him on the table and tried to make sense of all the scribbles.

"Is this the route we're taking?" she asked him, pointing to the line he had drawn in red. "Through the Green Forest?"

He didn't look up but continued to study the map. "No, Roark thinks we should take the New Road through Venari, but that won't get us there quickly and will just give anyone following time to catch up to us. We need to take this route, but we won't."

"Wouldn't the Green Forest take longer?" Aster asked.

"No, that's just it," Josiah replied, frustration lining his tone. "We can make it to Cedrus through these woods, refill any supplies in the main town, and grab a boat that will take us all the way down to Toparius. It's the quickest and safest route. But what do I know?" he said with a huff, throwing his hands up and pushing the map away in frustration.

Andi came up behind him and moved the map out of the way. "Josiah, don't act like that," she chided. "Roark has been doing this longer than you, and he believes the New Road is the best option for us. If he thinks it's the safest, then that's what we need to take. You need to trust him."

Josiah just crossed his arms and stared at the table in stony silence.

"Is it true the Green River is actually green?" Aster asked, trying to change the subject.

"It's very green," Andi answered. "Starting right here"—she pointed to a fork in the river—"the trees cover most of the river, allowing hardly any light to come through except in little spots here and there. So, instead of the water reflecting the sky, it reflects the green trees that cover it. I've only seen it a few times, but it's truly stunning, especially when the light shines through and hit's it, making it sparkle like an emerald."

"Isn't it dangerous, though? I've read stories about it in my books, and some of them are terrifying."

Andi scoffed. "Oh, those are just old wives' tales, meant to scare anyone from using it. The Evanders don't trust it, just like they don't trust us, so they made up stories about it to frighten people away."

Aster glanced at Josiah when Andi mentioned the Evanders. She wondered how hard it was for him to think about them now that she knew about his parents. He didn't seem affected by the comment, but he looked consumed by the maps in front of him. Despite his connection with Roark, she felt like there was an unspoken tension between them, and she wondered what exactly caused it.

She trusted Roark, for the most part, but Josiah's plan sounded like a reasonable one, especially if it meant avoiding the large, growing city of Venari.

Aster had heard stories of the place, and few of them were good. Stories of crime and poverty and the rich living it up in the hills, looking down upon those who were less fortunate. The city grew steadily thanks to the storms, and the Evanders of Veridi took advantage of the storms by expanding the city for their own gain and moving the capital of from Toparius to Veridi. She didn't necessarily like the idea of going through there. Josiah was right, Cedrus was more forest than town from the atlases she had looked at in the library. The river would be a great asset to get them quickly to Toparius.

"I agree with Josiah. I think the route through Cedrus makes more sense," Aster said, thinking out loud, and perfectly timed, too, for Roark entered the kitchen at just that exact moment.

"Josiah," Roark said, taking the maps from him and rolling them back up. "We've discussed this, and I don't believe we need to do so any further. We're taking the route through Venari, and that's final. You two need to trust me."

Josiah gave her a look. *Thanks, but it doesn't matter; Roark has the final say.*

She almost fell into the open seat. She had been able to read Josiah's look, and she somehow knew without a doubt that's what he was thinking.

As if she had read his thoughts.

She felt a pair of eyes studying her. Looking up, she saw Mag had stopped preparing breakfast and was staring at her intently. She must have felt Aster's powers reach a new level. But Mag turned around without a word, returning her focus to fixing breakfast.

As they ate in silence, Aster felt millions of questions vying for attention in her head. She figured now would be as good as any time to ask at least one, maybe two.

She chose what she hoped was an easy one. "Andi, what are the other powers you mentioned before? I know Nimuses, obviously."

"The others are Divums, who call themselves sky wielders, and Quarriers. Sky wielders can control things like the stars and clouds. Some of them can even control the weather. Quarriers can sense movements in the earth—"

"And cause them," Josiah interrupted with his mouth full.

Andi gave him a look but nodded, resigned. "He's right, sadly. The quarriers aren't the friendliest of people, but you aren't likely to meet any around here."

"Why?" Aster asked.

"Quarriers tend to stay in Gemma, sky wielders stay in Vela, and Nimuses reside here in Veridi."

When they finished eating, Roark gathered his bag and the maps. "It's time to go," he declared, before leaving the kitchen and walking out the front door.

Andi sighed. "I'm afraid he's right, Mag. Though I hate to leave you. What will you do when we leave? Will you be okay here by yourself?"

Mag laughed. "Child, I have been on my own long enough now. I will be fine, even if someone does show up. Why on earth would they suspect an old woman living off by herself? Just her and a garden, not even a sign of horses in the barn. Just a milk cow and a goat and chickens. No, I'll be quite fine, but I appreciate your concern, my dear." She placed a hand over Andi's.

"Mag, why don't you come with us?" Aster heard herself asking. She wasn't sure where the question had come from, but she didn't like the thought of going to the Academy and learning more about her future and past without Mag. She felt connected to this mysterious woman, even though she had only known her less than a day.

Mag stared at her, sadness filling her eyes. "My dear," she sighed, "I'm too old to make such a journey, even if I wanted to. This is where I'm meant to be, for now. One day, maybe sooner than we think, we might find ourselves together again, but right now I must stay here and watch for other travelers in need. When word spreads that the Light Keepers are on the verge of finding the Knight, they will be filled with hope and will make their way to the Academy to help."

Aster's shoulders slumped a little. Once again, she felt pressure at the idea of being part of the solution to defeating the darkness. It all felt so impossible, but every time her mind went down that path, she could hear the Knight's voice saying clearly, *"Go."*

Andi and Josiah said their goodbyes to Mag, grabbed their bags, and followed Roark outside, leaving Aster and Mag alone one last time. Aster's mind still pooled with so many questions for her, but she knew they didn't have time. She desperately hoped what Mag had said earlier was true, that they would all be together again. She figured Mag knew a lot more than she had told her in the short time they had talked.

Aster pushed away from the table and went over to Mag, who took her hands and gave them a squeeze.

"Aster," she said, staring at her intently."this journey ahead will be hard. There will be many unknowns and attacks that you will have to fight against. You'll be constantly bombarded with challenges and even experience sorrow." She paused, and Aster hung her head, concentrating on her shoes.

"But," Mag said, hope filling her voice, causing Aster to look back up at her, "you were born to succeed. You will find help when you least expect it. What seems impossible will be made possible. You will not be defeated unless you allow yourself to be. The Knight told you to go, and he wouldn't have unless he knew you could handle what's ahead. You'll know more soon enough, but go with what knowledge you have now, keep that journal close to you, and don't forget your purpose."

All Aster could do was nod. She didn't want to leave Mag or the safety of her cottage in the clearing behind, but she knew her destiny required her to go forward, not stand still, scared of the unknown. She gave Mag a long hug and whispered, "Thank you."

She grabbed the last backpack on the table, gave Mag one last look, and followed the others outside. The sky was already turning pink with the sunrise. Roark and Andi were mounted on their horses, leaving the dappled gray one for Aster to ride. She grimaced, not wanting to admit she wasn't the best on a horse, but she could manage. Josiah helped her up, and she settled down on the leather saddle, gripping the reins in her hands.

"Let's move out," Roark said, clicking his tongue and nudging his horse forward.

The others followed him, leaving the bright clearing, and entering the dark forest. Aster took one last look behind her at the cottage, and smiled when she saw Mag standing at the door, waving goodbye. She gave a little wave back, took a deep breath, and let herself and the horse be swallowed up by the thick trees and the heaviness of the unknown before them.

Chapter 7

The group made good progress, Roark seemed content with their pace, and he let them stop midafternoon to stretch their legs and water the horses.

They stopped not too far from a small, gurgling stream; Aster felt like it created a pretty scene she'd read in one of her books. She looked over and saw Josiah fiddling with the straps of his saddle, casting glances at Roark.

"Roark," Josiah said, "we're not too far off course. We could still choose the route through Cedrus. I know you think Venari is the best way, but it's not safe, trust me."

The way he said, "trust me," Aster believed Josiah had first-hand knowledge of the city. She realized he must have gone to Cedrus on missions to guard Light Keepers in need. Aster felt his thoughts battling against each other, his desire to listen to authority, yet the feeling in his gut that said Roark would regret taking them through the city well known for its seedy citizens.

She caught her breath; it was happening again. She realized when she stared at Josiah without looking away, she could feel what he was thinking. She'd always been able to read people, but this felt different from her usual perceptiveness. This felt like she was intruding.

She looked away, breaking the odd connection.

How? she wondered. *I thought I couldn't mind search without help from the Academy.*

Aster couldn't tell Josiah to skirt Roark's authority. Andi said he had been on this route many times. Aster wished she could shake the feeling that he was wrong, but she just couldn't. Maybe she needed to tell Andi how she felt. She wandered over to the stream, where Andi sat while her horse lapped up the cool water.

"Aster," Andi said, looking up at her with a smile, "how are you feeling?"

Aster stared at her, struggling to see her as the confidant she'd once been, but it was hard. Andi and Roark had become teachers to observe her; it made sense Andi had worked to become close to her. But it made Aster doubt the validity of their friendship.

"I'm sore, but I'm okay," was all she could get out.

Perhaps Andi wasn't her friend like she'd thought. Maybe she acted like a teacher and friend for her cover as a Light Keeper. Then it hit Aster like a lightning bolt—Roark and Andi were Light Keepers, meaning they had abilities like her. The weight of all her questions would push her down like a millstone around her neck if she didn't confide in someone. At this point, Andi was her only option.

Andi stared at her, and Aster could tell she knew something was wrong. She could always tell when Aster wasn't telling her everything.

Aster sighed. "I'm just so overwhelmed by everything." She plopped down, wrapping her arms around her knees. "Talking with Mag showed me a lot, but it also just gave me more questions that I don't have answers to, and I hate not knowing what's going on. Not to mention the pressure on me to help reunite a country."

Andi put her arm around Aster and pulled her close. "I know this all seems so scary, not knowing what's ahead, not knowing how you belong in this story yet, but you'll find a lot of your answers at the Academy, I promise. They'll be able to teach you so much there, and you'll discover a lot about yourself."

"What are your and Roark's abilities?" Aster asked, without thinking about it being polite or not.

Andi laughed. "I'm glad you asked." Lifting her hand up to the break in the trees above where they could see the sky, she moved her fingers in a funny motion and pulled her arm downward. As she did, Aster's eyes widened in surprise at the piece of cloud floating down towards Andi's hand. She held her palm flat, facing upward, allowing the tiny piece of cloud to hover over it.

"You're a sky wielder!" Aster exclaimed.

Andi smiled. "You can touch it," she said, nodding at the cloud in her hand.

Aster reached out and touched it gently with the tip of her finger.

"Oh!" she gasped. It felt like a pillow made of ice.

Andi laughed at her reaction and reached her hand down to the stream, letting go of the cloud. It evaporated once it left her hand and melted into the water.

"And Roark?" Aster asked.

"He's a Nimus, like you," Andi replied.

"How can we be sure I'm the right Nimus? It could be any of the others; I'm sure Gaia and Tarron had many descendants." Andi looked away and stared at the water, avoiding Aster's eyes. "We just know. There were signs and family trees we followed. I know everyone at the Academy is waiting for us to return with the Veridi heir. They've held on to hope for so long now." Andi added in a lighter tone, "You're a piece to an important puzzle, Aster."

Aster felt the sinking feeling in the pit of her stomach return.

At least I don't have to do it alone, she thought to herself. There were two others who had to share in this burden. Ignis was a large place, though. Trying to locate two more specific Light Keepers sounded like trying to find a needle in a haystack.

"I'm sorry. I know that just adds to your growing list of questions." Andi sighed. "One step at a time. Right now, we're in the journey step. The journey doesn't always make sense, and we often have to wait, but it's a necessary evil. Sometimes it can even be fun."

She leaned down towards the water, cupping some in her hands and tossing it on Aster.

Aster shook the cold, fresh water off, feeling wide awake now. She laughed and splashed Andi back, and soon they were laughing and soaking wet as the horses chomped on grass by the bed of the stream, bored with their riders.

"Stop it, both of you," Roark said from behind them. He stood there with his arms crossed, glaring at them both, but Aster could tell he was directing a good deal of his temper toward Andi. "We can't goof off. This is serious, and the fact that you're treating it like it's not worries me."

Aster realized she wasn't the target of his frustration at all.

"I think you know how seriously I take this. The fact you question my resolve even a little tells me so much," Andi said, shaking her wet hair out of her face. "I'm sorry if I wanted to ease the worries of this scared girl for just a second. If it weren't for your indecisiveness, Aster could have better prepared herself!"

Roark's nostrils flared, and they both just stared at each other as Andi's accusation hung between them like a fast-growing brick wall. Aster wondered who would move first, or if this staring contest would last forever. Roark huffed, turned, and stomped away, back through the brush they had come, Aster figured he was walking away before he spat back and created a wall between him and Andi permanently.

Andi sighed, her shoulders sagging. She stared off toward the stream and focused on an area far into the depths of the forest, trying to hide her emotions. Aster took her cue and walked away, dragging her horse unwillingly away from the refreshing water. She strode over to join Josiah, who stood with his back against a tree, studying at the maps he'd had out at Mag's.

"What was all the shouting?" Josiah asked.

"Oh, nothing," she said, trying to brush off the situation for Andi's sake, while also feeling the guilt surge once more for being the whole reason they were in this mess.

Josiah scoffed. "Yeah, sure." He saw through her fib. "It doesn't matter what Andi says. Roark always sees himself as right and others as wrong."

He put the map down a little, revealing his face, contorted with the conflict between his feelings that Aster had noticed earlier.

"I respect Roark, I do. I even look up to him, but lately he's been acting different. He's been more commanding, without compromise or willingness to listen to what anyone else has to say or contribute to solving the problems we're facing."

"You're so sure we shouldn't go through Venari, aren't you?" Aster asked.

"Yes, I am," he stated in a matter-of-fact tone. "I think it's foolish to walk through the open space between us and Venari. Cedrus is a safe route because it provides us more cover, especially with the Green River. I have a contact there in the village who could help us. Despite a couple vulnerable spots, we'd be safer compared to the New Road. Especially since we're being followed."

"We're being followed?" Aster asked in alarm.

Josiah looked like he wished he hadn't admitted it, but Aster would not let him get away easily.

"Josiah?"

"Yes," he sighed, rolling up his maps, avoiding her eyes. "I thought we had lost them at Mag's, but I noticed a few hours ago they found us again. I'm not sure who it is. They're keeping their distance but staying close enough to keep their sights on our trail."

"Does Roark know?" she asked, hating to bring him back up but knowing they couldn't keep him in the dark.

"Yes, I know," Roark's voice said from behind them.

Aster groaned and grimaced.

He always reappeared at the worst moment.

They swung around and stared at him.

"We are being followed, and that's why we can't waste time here anymore," Roark said, gathering the reins of his horse and pulling himself up. "Josiah, I know you don't trust my judgement in this, but your choice is to either continue with us or go back to Verd. Of course you abandoned your post there, which puts you on a watch list of deserters. I doubt that's a monster you want to face, but feel free if it seems like a better option than trusting me."

Aster could tell Roark's ultimatum stung Josiah, no matter how right he might be.

However, Roark left no room for interpretation or argument. Aster realized the only way she'd reach the Academy was through Roark. But she didn't know if she could handle his attitude towards her and the others. It was his way, or they were on their own, though Aster doubted Andi would just leave Josiah and her to fend for themselves.

But she also wasn't sure about anything anymore.

They set off without a word, riding for hours in the forest until they eventually reached the edge of the wood, where Aster could see open land ahead of them and a road winding east.

"It's too late in the day for us to travel in the open on the main road," Roark said, dismounting from his horse without warning. "We'll make camp here and start out first thing at dawn. Josiah, gather firewood and keep an eye out for anyone else who might be nearby. We're near enough to the main road, where we'll most likely begin encountering other travelers. We must be aware of their location and presence and avoid them as much as possible."

Without another word or instruction, Roark unsaddled his horse and stalked off to the edge of the forest to keep watch. Andi swung off her horse. Aster could tell her feelings were severely hurt after their argument. She felt Andi's guilt at calling Roark out on his mistake. Aster felt that odd feeling of connection she had felt earlier when deciphering Josiah's feelings, this time with Andi.

However, she didn't break it this time. She wanted to know how her friend was feeling, so she could best help her as Andi had helped Aster when she was dealing with hurt from friends and even family. Aster kept her eyes on Andi as she unsaddled her horse and began going through their provisions to make up dinner for them.

Whoosh. Aster suddenly heard muffled voices, like she had cotton stuffed in her ears. She didn't recognize from where or to whom they belonged. Over the muffled buzzing,

Andi's voice suddenly stood out among the rest. Aster could only understand a few words.

I can't believe I said that to him, said the voice... *In front of Aster, no less... so prideful... but he was wrong! But he wants.... safe...*

Aster heard this broken conversation from Andi, but she was looking straight at Andi and her mouth wasn't moving. She felt an odd sensation beginning in her fingertips, like her nerves were on fire, and the fire began spreading all over her.

What's happening to me?! Aster thought to herself, utterly terrified by the muffled noises, the clearness of what sounded like Andi's voice.

Is this the mind searching Mag mentioned? She realized, half relieved and half terrified. *She said I would need training for it... How is this possible?*

She glanced at Andi and saw horror and confusion written all over her face. She lost the sound of Andi's voice and heard only the muffled voices becoming louder and louder. The noise of it all hurt Aster's ears, like a swarm of bees stuffed inside. The fire coursed through her, sending shocks up and down her arms. She put her hands over her ears to stop the buzzing and tried brushing off the flames she was sure were engulfing her. It all became too much.

"AHH!" she yelled, doubling over and screaming out in pain.

As quickly as they came, the muffled voices dissipated. The heat of the flames died away and left her standing there, frightened and utterly exhausted.

She fell to her knees. Her eyes widened at the scorched ground beneath her hands, but for a moment she couldn't comprehend where the scorch marks had originated. The horses whinnied in fright, and Josiah had to calm them down as Andi and Roark rushed over to Aster, calling out to her. However, she noticed they weren't getting close.

"Aster." Andi said, trying to sound calming, but Aster could feel the panic and confusion laced in her tone, "Are you okay? Roark, what was that?" she asked him, the first time she had spoken to him since their argument at the stream.

"I don't know," Roark replied. "I've seen nothing like that. It's as if she was in one of her daydreams. But this, this was something much different. This was something dangerous."

"Did you see the sparks coming out of her hands?" Andi asked, her voice shaking.

"I did," was all Roark replied.

Aster didn't like how they were talking about her, like she wasn't there. She tried pushing herself up from the scorched ground, but when she tried to stand, her legs couldn't hold her. She wobbled, but before she could fall, Josiah caught her with one hand, steadying her on her feet. She glanced up at him, reading his expression, and all she saw was concern— not fear, like she saw from Andi and Roark.

"Aster," Roark said, getting her attention. "Can you tell us anything about what led up to your episode?"

Aster looked away from Josiah and tried to train her eyes on Roark, but whatever happened had caused her to experience vertigo, and she was doing her best to keep everything from spinning.

I need to tell them about the voices, she thought to herself.

Not to mention the very real fire she'd felt. The scorched earth beneath her hands was proof enough.

Yet, she couldn't bring herself to explain any of it, not after seeing Roark and Andi's faces and hearing the fear in their voices.

"No," she replied, "I don't know what happened. I was just daydreaming and quickly felt winded, and that's when I fell, I guess."

She wanted it to sound as normal, for her, as possible, but she could tell Roark didn't entirely believe her. Aster knew their reaction meant it must have looked as bad from their vantage point as it had felt from hers.

He studied her for another moment, then sighed. "I suppose it's just as Mag said. Her ability will continue to grow with time. Though it's advancing quicker than expected," he said. "Therefore, we need to get to the Academy as soon as possible. Josiah, help her to that tree and Andi will look after her, then go scout the perimeter and gather firewood. Don't forget to keep away from any other travelers…"

Aster could feel Josiah stiffen beside her, but she knew it wasn't because of Roark's attitude this time, because she saw what he did, and knew that Roark's plan to keep a low profile had gone out the window. A rough group of men and women were standing behind him, staring at them. Aster noticed they all had one thing in common, other than their grubby appearance.

They were all armed to the hilt with weapons.

Chapter 8

Roark spun around, taking in their unexpected guests. Aster could tell his mind was working to count and assess their possibility of escape. Josiah reached to unsheathe his sword, but Roark motioned for him to stop.

"Wait," Roark muttered.

"Hello." He moved to greet the large party of weapon-carrying travelers. "We're sorry if we disturbed you and your camp. One of our group slipped and fell. She's not been well. We're taking her to Venari to see a doctor. If you need this space, we'll readily move along. Our party is much smaller than yours, and I'm sure you could use the area to spread out."

Aster knew he was trying to defuse the situation and appear vulnerable, but she hoped he also had a plan in mind in case this didn't work. She had seen Roark settle the fights at school, and he always tried to calm the situation before resorting to physical methods. The times he had used physical methods, she remembered being surprised at how skilled in combat he was for a headmaster. Despite his ruse, she could sense the large group of weapon carriers wasn't about to stand down and shake hands.

"Oh, my, I hope the lass is okay," the leader said. At least, Aster figured he was the leader.

He wore an expensive-looking green leather coat with bright gold-leafed buttons. Aster also noticed all had a similar emblem etched on the front of their clothing. It looked like a dog, and something about it felt eerily familiar to Aster.

Then she remembered.

The realization hit her like a brick, knocking the air out of her.

She felt her heart pounding and her mouth open in a wordless cry.

She took a step closer to Josiah and grabbed his sleeve. He

looked down at her, questioning, but she kept her eyes forward, looking straight at the intimidating group in front of them. She discreetly put her hand over her heart, hoping he would look and see the emblem etched into the leather of the leader's coat.

The men and women standing before them did not show mercy, nor did they allow their victims to go without a fight.

They were mercenaries. Not just any mercenaries. These were the Cu-Sith. Their stories were ones that gave Aster nightmares growing up.

The stories said the Cu-Sith, when not commissioned by the Evanders, used the storms to prey on innocent people, attacking them as they fled for their lives. They seldom left any survivors, and they lived on their spoils in the empty wastelands created by the storms. Once their supplies became low or another group fled from a storm, they'd leave and attack again. They were like storms themselves, not having a care for human life.

Aster knew it would be a miracle if they made it out with their supplies, let alone their lives. She cast a fearful glance at Roark but couldn't tell if he knew Cu-Sith surrounded them. She wondered how much of her episode the Cu-Sith had witnessed.

Joke is on them, though, she thought to herself. *I have no clue what happened.*

She hadn't even made it to the Academy yet. It might be she wasn't the Flower with a Royal Mind. Perhaps she was just a freak who the Light Keepers wanted to believe was one key to finding the Knight.

"What kind of illness is it? We have our own physician with us, who I'm sure could help," the leader said. "Why don't you bring her over here?"

Josiah immediately pulled Aster behind him. A few Cu-Sith slowly spread out behind him, forming a circle around Aster and the others.

Roark played along, though; Aster hoped he was trying to keep the leader talking as long as possible, so he could create a plan to get them out of this alive.

"I wish I knew. I don't think it's contagious, but I can't promise that. It's better if she stays with us, just in case. She's exposed me and my group already; I highly advise you all to keep your distance. You wouldn't want to catch whatever she has. It seems deadly."

The Cu-Sith leader laughed. "Oh, I don't think it's anything we can catch. But it is something we can stop."

It all happened so fast; the Cu-Sith leader lunged at such a speed he seemed to fly. His hand reached out toward her, curled as if ready to grab her by the throat. Roark flung himself forward, intercepting the man, and they both fell in a heap to the ground. Meanwhile, the rest of the group quickly formed a tighter circle around Josiah, Andi, and Aster, leaving no time for Josiah to push Andi and Aster away to safety. Aster saw the faces of the Cu-Sith clearer now. She couldn't believe her own eyes. Their skin looked pinched and pulled, as if it didn't quite fit right.

Josiah held his sword out now and was trying to keep Andi and Aster covered, but it was no use. The Cu'Sith had them surrounded. He lunged to draw their attention to him, but all he did was nick one of them, and Aster noticed that the Cu-Sith's skin flaked off, revealing something that wasn't blood.

Instead, she saw a strange-looking flesh below the flap that dangled off his arm where Josiah had attacked him.

What are these people? she thought, horrified.

Roark and the Cu-Sith leader were wrestling each other, the leader seemed to have a firm upper hand as he slammed Roark to the ground, but Roark wasn't giving up, either. Aster noticed again that surprising stamina and strength she had seen at school when he broke up fights between students. He tried, but he couldn't take the leader down, ending up in a choke hold. The leader lifted him up and kept one arm tightly around his neck while the other held a knife with a black, shining handle and various spikes poking out at random points.

"Okay, now, everyone, calm down." He pointed to Aster, keeping his other arm tight across Roark's throat as he struggled.

"You, girl," he said, nodding toward her. "Come here. We don't have to hurt your friends. We just want you."

What could they possibly want her for? Did they know what she was? And what did he mean by something they could stop? Were they trying to stop the Light Keepers from finding the

Knight?

"Why do you need me?" she asked, trying to sound brave. She hoped if she could get him talking long enough, she could free Roark.

"Because you're dangerous. You're highly valuable to an interested party that's paid us to come this far inland to search for you. I thought we had missed out when we couldn't find you at your home. Nice library, by the way."

Aster's stomach dropped, and her knees almost buckled. Her blood boiled at the thought of these monsters in her house, in her family library! She desperately hoped her family had made it safely out of Verd, but she couldn't let herself think about it or she would collapse in a heap right here.

"I don't know why someone would want me. I'm no one important," she said with a stronger voice. "Like he said, I'm sick. No one knows what's wrong with me, but that's why we're out here traveling. And as for whatever town and house you searched, it surely wasn't mine. The place I once called home didn't even have a library, and I hate books." She winced inwardly, hoping he couldn't see through her lie.

The leader laughed again, causing the hair on Aster's arms to stand up. This laugh was more menacing than before, and she realized his patience was thinning. She had to be careful to not incite him.

"You're not a talented liar, lass," he said. "Come here, and we might not scrape up your friends too badly." He laughed again, and so did his fellow monsters, though Aster thought theirs sounded more like hisses.

"You're not a talented liar, either," Aster replied boldly. "You have the upper hand. I know you'll kill them the minute I come over to you and you take me for whatever bounty someone set on me. I think before that happens, because I realize it will, I deserve to know why you and your employer think I'm so valuable."

During this exchange, her mind was working overtime, but she needed him to keep talking. She had to try.

He studied her, trying to see through any trick she might try to play. Thankfully, she had been completely truthful this time.

He and his monsters did have the upper hand. He nodded. "Fine…"

He began talking, but Aster tuned him out. She focused on Roark. She pooled all her concentration on getting him to realize her plan. He seemed to catch on, and he blinked twice to let her know he'd be ready. She knew it's what he meant because she had formed a connection as she had done with Andi and Josiah earlier. She kept the connection, going until the leader's voice became muffled, and everything sounded like she had her head in a bucket again. Keeping her gaze on Roark, she could feel the fire snaking up her arms from the palms of her hands. The muffled voices filled her ears once more, but it was all just noise to her. She focused singularly on Roark and his thoughts, and they came in slices like Andi's.

You can… hit the ground…

Josiah… Andi… You can…

She took a deep breath, smelling the smoke hanging in the air, growing thicker and thicker. The leader stopped talking, but the hissing echoed in her ears. The buzzing from earlier grew extremely painful—she almost couldn't stand it—but she needed to hold on for another minute at least. Finally, she couldn't stand the pain any longer. She also had no clue what would happen if she continued to hold the connection with Roark a moment longer.

NOW! she heard him think, as if shouting at her.

Aster forced herself to end the connection. A loud *pop* sounded, and she fell to the ground. She heard Roark yelling for Josiah to run. Suddenly, she felt herself lifted off the ground and flung onto the back of a horse. Aster gasped and her eyes went wide as a rough hand grabbed her ankle.

White-hot pain soared up her leg. The owner of the hand howled in agony, immediately letting go of her.

She heard Josiah say something that sounded like, "Hold on, Aster!"

Then the world went black.

Aster woke up under a canopy of trees towering high above her head. Their large, green leaves created a cover, casting odd shadows, allowing only slivers of light to escape and fall on her.

The hard earth under her didn't help the aches covering her from head to toe. She struggled to lift herself off the ground; moaning, she realized the excretion proved to be too much for her yet.

"Careful," a nearby voice cautioned.

She glanced over to her right and saw Josiah, maps laid out in front of him, and their horse tied to a tree next to him.

His eyes were weary, and his hair mussed from running his hands through it in frustration.

How long had she been asleep?

Where were they?

Where were Roark and Andi?

The simple task of asking questions felt like climbing a mountain to her. The world spun a little, causing her stomach and head to feel unbalanced.

"Yeah, you'll want to take it easy for the moment," Josiah cautioned again, keeping his gaze roaming over the maps. "We can't rest for too long. We need to make up the time we've lost. Plus, who knows what else we might encounter? I think that now we're on the right path, we might avoid any unwelcome encounters. I want to arrive at base of The Cedrus mountains by evening."

Aster's head turned too quickly to look at him. "Wait, what do you mean, the Cedrus Mountains? What happened to going through Venari?"

She glanced around, feeling as if something was missing.

Dread filled her stomach.

"Josiah, what's going on? Where are Roark and Andi?"

She gingerly scooted herself to a sitting position and leaned against the trunk of the tree behind her.

Josiah kept his eyes on the map, running his hands through his hair again, gripping it with so much force she thought he might pull chunks of it out.

"Josiah!" she said again, as forcefully as possible in her present condition.

He glanced at her and just shrugged his shoulders.

"What?" he asked.

Her eyes widened at the tone in which he'd responded.

He sounded as if they hadn't just run from a gang of Cu-Sith. He sounded like he hadn't just watched her create a fire with her body, not once but twice.

"What do you mean, 'what?'" she asked incredulously. He sighed, putting his head in his hands. "Fine. I honestly don't know what happened back there. It all happened so quickly, and it was like nothing I've ever seen before."

He stood up and moved closer to her, his eyes refusing to meet hers.

"They had us surrounded. I noticed you looking at Roark like you did with Andi before your first episode," he said, as though uncertain what else to call the phenomenon. "I figured something might happen. I tried to ready myself, but the shock almost took me down.

"Your plan worked at first because their leader dropped Roark, and he was able to grab his knife and defend himself. You had collapsed, and he knew the important thing was to get you free. He yelled at me to get you out of there. I put you on the horse and bolted. I tried to grab Andi, but she stayed behind to help Roark. I knew she would. Even knowing that, I feel terrible leaving her."

He stopped.

But she wanted to know more.

"Why are we headed toward Cedrus? If Roark and Andi made it out." Her voice caught. "Won't they follow the original path, thinking they'll catch up to us? But now we won't be there!"

Josiah stiffened at her accusatory tone. She didn't regret her words, though. Aster believed he'd seized advantage of the situation. He'd made it clear before their attack how convinced he was that Roark's path was the wrong way. Now was his chance to prove it. She felt bad questioning his intentions, but she felt so unsure about everything at the moment.

"Yes, I know how to get there. I've studied these maps, and I used to live at the Academy, remember? I know Cedrus is the right path," he said with conviction. "We'll be the safest once we reach the village. Once we're there, we'll buy a boat and be on the river by nightfall. Once we're on the river, we'll be safe.

Much safer than going through Venari.

"You've heard the stories of the Venari streets," he continued to defend his choice. "They're not safe, and I knew they'd be even worse for us without Andi or Roark. I truly hope they made it out, and knowing them, they probably did. And knowing Roark, he'd probably realized what I would do if given the chance."

Aster didn't respond. She was trying to decide how to feel.

She felt angry toward Josiah for taking chances because he was so sure he was right.

She felt worried sick about Andi and Roark's fate. She battled the most with feeling guilt. The notion of being someone special had felt nice in the safety of Mag's garden. But she didn't want to be special anymore if this is what it meant.

"Ugh," she said, leaning her head against the rough-barked tree. "This is all so messed up. I should be back home, reading instead of doing homework, helping with the evening chores, and getting lost in another daydream. I should be outside, my brother yelling at me to focus and help instead of nodding off in the clouds." She tried to keep the tears at bay, but they pooled at her eyes and trickled down her cheeks.

After meeting Mag, she had felt more hopeful, even in the face of the unknown. When she thought of losing Andi and Roark, she felt overwhelmed.

"I hope you're right about Cedrus," she mumbled.

She felt Josiah's arm drop over her shoulders, a little tentatively but also strong, like he was trying to help hold her up against the onslaught of feelings.

"Please, Aster, it will be okay. I want you to trust me. I know I'm not as experienced as Roark or comforting like Andi." She laughed a little at his attempt to lighten the mood. "But I will protect you, and I will get us to the Academy in one piece. I won't let anyone hurt you."

The tone in his voice caused her heart to skip a little, and she could feel a blush creeping across her cheeks. Brushing the tears away, she raised her head, turning away from Josiah until she could feel her cheeks return to normal color. "More like any*thing* rather than anyone," she said with a harsh laugh. "The Cu-Sith will keep hunting for me. I've only heard stories about them, but those stories are mild compared to the reality. They didn't look fully human, if that makes sense."

Josiah shrugged, taking his arm off Aster's shoulders. "I'm not sure what they were, but I'm almost positive they weren't actually Cu-Sith. Whatever they are, I got the distinct feeling you're right. They weren't human. Especially that one…"

He stopped himself mid-sentence, glancing away from her. He stood up and went back to his maps.

"What?" she asked. "What were you about to say?"

He didn't answer at first, fiddling with the map in his hands, weighing his thoughts before speaking. "I don't know if you remember, but one of them grabbed your ankle as we tried to ride off, but the moment he did…" Josiah paused.

"What, Josiah? What happened?" She couldn't remember what happened clearly, just blacking out. But suddenly a glimpse of memory slipped back into her mind's eye and her breath quickened.

Josiah looked at her questioningly, watching the memory slowly return to her. She couldn't bring herself to voice what she'd seen. She looked at him, hoping he would say it instead. He sighed.

"When he grabbed your ankle, it was like a shock went through you. He screamed and let go, with his skin burnt off." Josiah pushed a hand roughly through his hair again.

That must be a nervous habit for him, Aster realized.

"His hand withered up, like dead grass. The others stayed back after that happened. It scared them to come near you, which helped us escape."

"I remember now," she whispered.

She felt the white-hot pain on her ankle. There was no evidence on her skin to show what had happened, but she felt it inside her very soul. She rubbed her ankle, remembering the feel of the rough hand on her skin, the shock that went through her, and his hand releasing.

Her desire to reach the Academy grew, and new questions swirled in her head. Did all mind searchers experience episodes like hers? She recalled the frightened looks on Andi's and

Roark's faces, which made her inclined to believe it was not normal.

Andi was right, she thought to herself. *I have to read the journal in order to learn more about my power.*

"The journal!" she cried out frantically, searching around for the precious book.

"It's okay!" Josiah said quickly, showing her the bag she had been carrying. "I grabbed it the moment you freed Roark."

He handed her the bag, and she opened it to take out the journal. The journal anchored her emotions, and she felt her shoulders relax.

"I do trust you, Josiah," she whispered, running her hand across the soft leather of the journal.

He hadn't kept his distance when things got strange. If he could trust her after her unexplainable episode, she could trust him to get them safely to Toparius and the Academy.

He glanced at her and gave a grateful smile. "Okay, well," he said. "Eat and rest, but not for long. We have to leave as soon as possible. I'm sorry I can't let you rest more, but we have a good day's ride ahead of us."

Her body ached, but she also understood the need for urgency. She was ready to be in safer territory. He rolled up his maps as she ate a few bites of what little food they had left. Sadly, the rest of the supplies were on Andi's horse. Aster hoped they had enough to make it to Cedrus.

After a few minutes, Josiah indicated it was time to leave. They mounted their shared horse and took their time through the brush and the trees.

"I've never been this far from home before," Aster commented, feeling a sense of awkwardness growing between them amid their proximity to each other.

"Really?" Josiah asked. "I guess I'm not surprised. The Evanders don't like their people to travel back and forth. It opens up the opportunity for groups of like-minded people to grow, and they don't trust that there won't be a group, or groups, who may oppose them."

"You don't like the Evanders, do you?" she asked, sensing a deep well of bitterness coming from Josiah's tongue every time he mentioned their name.

"They're an overbearing government of men and women who believe they should be in control. They took over Ignis after the earthquakes, and I know they're partly to blame for my parents' deaths."

"I'm sorry, Josiah. I can't imagine how hard that was on you."

Josiah nodded but remained quiet, and Aster felt guilty for bringing up his parents, which fell so heavily on his shoulders. She reached up and put her hand on his shoulder to comfort him. He looked back at her hand and smiled, reaching up and placing his own on top of hers.

Aster hadn't meant to create a moment, but it happened nonetheless. An awkward tension suddenly grew between them. They both seemed to sense it, because their hands dropped, and Aster put hers back around his waist to keep herself from falling off the horse. Though she realized that didn't help matters much.

The silence eventually became comfortable again, and Aster realized the trees were growing taller the farther they rode. Josiah finally found a path leading up the mountain, which gave Aster a sense of comfort, knowing they were headed in the right direction. However, she also realized her vulnerability in these surroundings when she realized the tree trunks were so wide anyone or anything could hide behind them. All she could picture for hours were groups of Cu-Sith hiding behind one of the wood giants, just waiting to pounce on them.

Eventually it became too dark for them to continue onward, but Josiah seemed pleased with their progress.

"We should reach Cedrus tomorrow. My contact there will help us replenish our supplies and buy a boat."

They munched on pieces of the meager remains of their food supplies, and Aster fell asleep almost immediately afterward, not having enough strength to volunteer to help keep watch. They started out early the next day, since neither of them could stay asleep. Aster tossed and turned all night. Dreams of Cu-Sith and Andi and Roark crying out for help attacked her the minute she closed her eyes. She woke in a sweat, and their cries for help echoed in her mind, sending a chill down her spine.

They climbed up the mountain under thick foliage, surrounded by a heavy canopy of fog, making it so dark Aster didn't know if it was day or night. Thankfully, Josiah seemed to sense the time and their location, because he eventually slowed down.

"We're almost there," he stated with relief as they crested a steep incline.

An hour later, Aster saw smoke rising ahead of them, and as they got closer, she realized it was coming from chimneys. She suddenly realized she would finally see a place she had only ever read about in her books. Her heart thrilled at the thought of visiting a new town, and her heart felt lighter than it had since they started their journey. Yet, her books hadn't prepared her for what her eyes saw.

Chapter 9

As they approached Cedrus, Aster felt like a bug, with the tall trees towering above her like blades of grass. The bark on the trees was green, and they towered above her head so high that she hurt her neck, straining to see where they ended.

They have to be touching the sky, she thought in wonder.

They called Cedrus the City of Trees for a reason. The trees served as the houses, shops, taverns, and Aster even saw a school fixed inside the round hollow of a trunk farther up the road. The tree houses were intricately woven together, connected by wooden bridges here and rope bridges there. The people themselves looked like the trees they lived and worked in. She almost didn't see them because of their dress of camouflage and the green streaks on any exposed skin.

"Why do they look green?" she whispered to Josiah. Aster felt eyes of many unseen faces trained on them as they traveled through the city.

"They wear camouflage and streak their skin with chlorophyll powder to keep safe," he whispered back. "If the Evanders or Cu-Sith try to attack them, the people can hide in plain sight. Giving them the advantage. It's always a little unnerving at first, but you get used to it," he added, looking up and around at the bustling citizens.

Aster doubted she would, but they wouldn't be here long, anyway. Yet, she found herself drawn to this place and its unique lifestyle.

She couldn't help smiling, remembering back to when she and her siblings had played in a tree house their father had built for them. She could picture the day he'd finished it…

Sawdust had still covered the wood-planked floors when they'd rushed to see the final product. She'd raced with her brothers and little sister to the tree house. "Wait for me!" she yelled after them.

They always seemed to forget to include her on exciting adventures like this.

Amity had squealed when she looked over the edge. "Look, Aster! Look how high up we are!"

At their young age, it had felt like they were in the clouds. The four of them had played in the tree for hours until their mother called to say it was time for dinner.

The minute they'd cleared their plates, they'd asked in unison, "May we be excused to go play in the tree house?"

"Yes, go," their father had laughed.

"Don't get too close to the edge!" their mother warned.

Laughing, the four of them had run outside to the tree house and shimmied up the ladder. Aster remembered having a clear view of the beautiful sun setting itself down for the day in a fluffy white cloud blanket.

They'd played in the tree house every day after morning chores, before dinner, and after, till the stars began twinkling in the sky.

One starry night, Amity and Aster had sat with their legs dangling off the edge, looking up into the sea of stars above them.

Laying down on her back, Amity had sighed happily, "Aster, when we grow up, let's live in a tree house!"

Aster had laughed. "In this tree house?"

"No, a really big one, with maybe a couple of rooms. Father will build it! We'll live in it and build higher—with a tower at the top, like a castle!"

Aster loved when her sister's imagination was as active as her own. "It would be fun to live in a tree house."

She'd smiled and stared up into the sky. She'd imagined a huge tree house with so many levels it reached the top. Her imagination had begun exploding with fantastic dreams of what it would be like to live in a tree.

Aster couldn't remember much afterward; other than that their father had torn down the tree house. Their mother had said it was too dangerous and had their father dismantle it. She remembered her siblings being visibly angry with her, but she couldn't remember exactly why. It wasn't like it had been her fault the tree house had to be taken down.

Or had it been?

A chill went down her spine as dread filled her.

"Aster," she heard her name being called, but she couldn't seem to answer.

"Aster. Aster!" Josiah hissed.

She startled and almost spooked the horse. She glanced and saw Josiah standing below her, off the horse, trying to get her attention without yelling and drawing too much attention from others. He looked at her with confusion, and worry knitted his brows.

"I'm sorry," she apologized quietly. "How long was I out?"

"Not long. But, Aster, I struggled to get you back this time," he said with concern.

"I'm sorry," she said again. "It was the tree houses; they sparked a memory of me and my siblings, when my father built us a tree house. But Josiah, something's wrong," she added in a whisper. "I'm realizing more and more that my memories aren't complete."

"What do you mean?" he asked curiously.

"It's like I'm only seeing parts of the story. I just keep getting the feeling something isn't right."

Aster shuddered. She recalled Mag's warning that she shouldn't push for the memories to return.

"When you do, you might not like what you find," Mag had warned ominously.

"Let's set up camp somewhere. I'm sure you just need more rest," he said, glancing around, hoping a place would show itself.

She highly doubted that, but maybe. It was then she realized she hadn't slept soundly for a few days now, not since the last time she slept in her own bed. Each night's sleep had been restless or nonexistent since they couldn't make long stops.

Carefully, she swung herself off the horse, stretching her legs, hoping that might get the blood flowing and keep her awake.

"Surely there's somewhere, maybe an inn?" She didn't exactly love the idea of camping out in unfamiliar territory.

They both looked around. Josiah realized they were attracting attention and motioned to her, they needed to keep moving so as not to seem suspicious.

"Hello there!" said a voice behind them.

They turned to see a smiling little girl staring up at them. Aster figured she was six, maybe seven, but the girl's enormous eyes and toothy smile gave Aster's heart a lurch, reminding her of her little sister Amity when she was that age.

"Well, hello," Aster replied, bending down, so she was eye level with the little girl.

"I'm Morgan! You all aren't from here," she blurted. Before Aster could respond, the girl continued,"We don't get a lot of visitors here, but my family runs the inn down the road. Do you need a place to stay?"

Josiah stubbornly shook his head, and Aster tried to let the girl go gently, but Morgan grabbed her hand and pulled her away.

"Come on! You'll love it! You can have our nicest room. Since we don't have any other guests, but also because I like you! You look like a princess."

She stopped and spun to face Aster so hastily Aster almost fell over her. Aster felt uncomfortable under the little girl's stare, although she was sure she meant well. It almost felt like Morgan knew Aster was not quite normal.

Aster smiled, trying to deflect Morgan's attention. "Thank you so much, but you're the one who looks like a princess," she said pleasantly, touching the girl's intricately braided hair with green ribbon laced in it.

Morgan gave her toothy smile, twirled back around, and continued to pull Aster along. Aster looked back helplessly at Josiah and shrugged. She sensed he was not happy, but she didn't want to be rude to the girl or her family. He shrugged back and pulled the horse along, following close behind, trying to keep up with the little girl, whose short legs were fast.

The girl led them through a little market, where passersby waved and said hello to Morgan, giving odd looks to the two newcomers she dragged in her wake.

"Come on, we're almost there!" Morgan said in a sing-song voice.

Morgan stopped abruptly, causing Aster to stumble this time.

"There it is! The Garden Inn. It's called The Garden because of my mother's gardens around the house."

It was obvious as to the reason for its name, and Aster was in awe of the beautiful, colorful array of flowers surrounding the large tree house inn.

This almost rivals Mag's garden, she thought to herself.

The inn looked like a painting. A little two-story house with a thatched roof and curved windows laced with beautiful ivy sat in front of a tall, green-barked tree. They moved closer, and Aster realized it must have been one of the hollowed-out trees, because the part attached to the house had little windows winding up its trunk, with flower boxes sitting on the window ledges.

Aster's eyes filled with tears, thinking of what her sister's reaction would be to the beautiful tree house. She blinked away the tears, glancing down at Morgan. The girl beamed up at her proudly.

This is the best tree house ever.

Aster gasped, realizing she had read Morgan's thoughts, like she had Josiah's, Andi's and Roark's.

She shook her head, trying to focus on the present.

"Well, I'm not wrong, isn't the best tree house ever?" Morgan remarked innocently.

Aster's heart-beat fast inside her throat. Did Morgan know Aster had heard her thoughts?

A petite, graceful-looking woman came out of the house before Aster could fully comprehend their interaction. She had flour on her hands, which she wiped across her green apron. Aster noticed the woman's hair and face looked very similar to the little girl. Morgan followed Aster's eyes and ran to the woman.

"Momma! Momma!" she cried, grabbing the woman's hand and dragging her towards Aster and Josiah.

"Look! New people! And they need a place to stay. I told them we'd give them the best room because no one else is here. And doesn't she look like a princess, Momma?"

Aster wondered how the mother kept up with her vivacious, talkative daughter every day. She was obviously used to it, though, nodding and taking the whirlwind of information as it came. Placing her hand on Morgan's shoulder, she looked at her and said calmly, "Morgan, tell your father to prepare two extra places for dinner, and make sure the rooms are ready for them.

Okay?"

"Okay, Momma!" Morgan said, snapping to attention and running to the cottage. "See ya later!" she yelled back at her new friends.

The mother laughed and sighed. "I'm sorry about that. Morgan becomes excited whenever someone new comes to town. It certainly doesn't happen that often."

"No need to apologize. I wish I had her level of energy and excitement." Aster laughed. "I'm Aster, and this is Josiah. We're just passing through, and-."

"Josiah?"

Josiah carefully studied the woman. "Yes," he replied, unsure why this woman would know him.

"He said you might stop here, but it was just wishful thinking. So many go through Venari now. He'll be so happy to see you!"

Josiah and Aster glanced at each other, confused and a little apprehensive. How did she know they were coming?

"I'm sorry," Josiah eventually managed, "how do you know me? And who told you I might come?"

"Oh, look at me getting ahead of myself, I'm so sorry." she held out a hand to him. "I'm Flora, Collin's wife."

Josiah's eyes widened, and he stood speechless. Finally, he snapped back into focus and shook her hand heartily, a big smile spreading across his face.

"I can't believe it! Collin, married!"

He pulled her into a big hug, and Aster became even more confused.

"Where is he?" Josiah asked after putting her down.

"He's inside cooking dinner! I'm a terrible cook, so I was happy to give him the role."

Josiah laughed. "Of course! I remember he taught me how to cook when he was home at the Academy. His venison stew was my favorite! Has he ever made it for you?"

"Meat isn't a common commodity in the area. Collin has gotten good at cooking vegetable dishes, and he's tried all different methods of cooking potatoes." Flora laughed.

Aster cleared her throat a little to remind them both she was still standing there in the dark. Josiah glanced at her and realized his error in manners.

"Oh, Aster, I'm sorry," he said. "Collin is the contact I mentioned. He lived and worked at the Academy when I grew up there, after my parents, well, you know. I never imagined finding him the owner of an inn, let alone married with children."

"How else can a man provide a place for his friend to stay when he visits?" A man stood in the inn's doorway, his arms crossed and a smirk on his face. He and Josiah rushed to greet each other with a brotherly hug.

"Look who the cat dragged in!" Collin said, holding Josiah out at arm's-length.

"Look who got married and settled down!" Josiah teased.

"Well, she wouldn't stop pestering me, so I finally had to comply. Became a businessman and finally asked her to marry me." He laughed, winking at Flora, who put her hands on her hips and arched her eyebrow.

"Excuse me!" she said in mock surprise. "I believe you persuaded me to say yes to you?"

Collin winced but shrugged. "Well, can you blame me for pursuing you?"

"No, I can't." she smarted back with a smirk.

Aster liked the couple already.

"Hello! Don't tell me you're Josiah's wife?" Collin smiled and shook her hand warmly.

Josiah's face reddened. Aster felt her eyes almost pop out of her head.

"No, no!" she said quickly, too quickly, apparently, because Josiah gave her a look.

"Ouch," he said, putting his hand over his heart as if she broke it. "Thanks for making me feel good about myself."

"No! I'm sorry. I didn't mean it like that!" feeling like she was digging a deeper hole.

Flora swatted Collin on the back of his head. "Collin, don't embarrass these two!"

Collin rubbed his head w and laughed. "I'm sorry. I'm sorry, I shouldn't have assumed. I figured you weren't, anyway. Josiah has always made it clear he doesn't want that kind of life."

Aster looked at Josiah, who threw dagger-eyes at his friend.

"I didn't say that exactly."

Collin scoffed, but Flora gave him a look to stop the conversation.

"Well, you're both welcome here, of course! For however long you need to stay," Flora said, steering the conversation to an alternate path.

"Thank you so much," Aster replied.

"Why don't I take you to your room?" Flora offered Aster.

"That would be wonderful, thank you," Aster replied, following Flora, leaving Josiah behind without a second glance. She felt so silly for having reacted like that to Collin's assumption, but ever since they'd talked in Mag's garden under the starry sky, and their moment while riding, she felt this awkwardness between her and Josiah.

Aster found him attractive. She just felt already overwhelmed with change. She didn't think she could handle anymore. Plus, she didn't know how he felt. He was so closed off sometimes. He rarely showed his emotions clearly, especially to her. She shook her head free from the situation and Josiah and instead tried focusing on the inn as she followed Flora inside.

"It's beautiful!" she exclaimed. She had barely crossed the threshold, but the beauty of this tree house inn immediately took her breath away. The house portion, which they entered through, had a beautifully carved wooden chandelier that cast a halo of light on the polished wood floor. The dining room held a large wooden table in the middle of the room, gleaming as brightly as the floors. The straight-backed chairs each had an intricately carved design of various woodland creatures on the back. Aster's favorite chair depicted a hare, the animal of Veridi, sitting tall in the middle of a field of wildflowers. The detail in the carving almost gave the feeling the hare's whiskers twitched and the flowers moved in the breeze.

"Who made these?" Aster asked in awe.

"Collin did," Flora replied, beaming with pride for her clearly talented husband. "He's a carpenter and built most of the furniture for the inn. He also built on the additions to the tree house when we bought it."

"Who owned it before you all?" Aster asked, following Flora past a small parlor that looked out into the garden.

"My parents," Flora replied, turning to climb up the stairs opposite the parlor. "They opened it before I was born, back when people traveled through Cedrus more often. When they became unable to care for it anymore, Collin knew how much I loved it growing up and how I wanted the same experience for my children. He offered to run it—well, he offered that we *both* run it. His job is to cook the meals. He also built on to the outside of it and bought the tree house next door to give us more room. My job was to fix up the garden to its former glory, mother once had it, we haven't had guests for quite some time," she added with a bitter undertone.

She seemed to regret her tone and promptly explained herself. "I'm sorry, it's just that with the storms and the Evanders expanding the Venari city line, we've struggled to find travelers looking for a place to stay. When they changed the route to Toparius to run through Venari instead of Cedrus, we lost a lot of business. If you could have seen this place when my parents ran it! People from all over traveled through Cedrus."

She sighed. "Enough of that talk, though. Let's go upstairs to your room, and we'll get you settled."

Aster felt dazed by the quick change in Flora's attitude and the direction of their conversation. She didn't know why the Evaders had changed the route or why they continued to push the boundaries of Venari. Flora seemed to know, and Aster wondered why she didn't voice it.

Josiah said the Evanders have been trying to wipe out the Light Keepers. Is Cedrus connected to the Light Keepers? Aster thought to herself.

"Aster?" Flora asked, breaking her out of her thoughts.

Aster felt her heart race and heat rush to her face.

How long had she been out? Evidently not long, but Flora's face informed her it was long enough to cause concern.

"I'm so sorry," Aster covered up. "I became distracted by this beautiful staircase and the mural on the wall! Is Collin an artist, too?"

If Flora could change subjects, so could she.

Flora continued to stare at her closely, but released her gaze and looked at the wall, smiling. "No, Collin's artwork is carpentry. I painted the walls."

"They're beautiful," Aster said, trying to take in the entire mural, which stretched up the wall following the staircase. "Your talents sound well suited to each other."

Flora smiled, running her hand across the banister. "Yes, I'm glad I found Collin. He needed me, and I needed him."

Aster smiled, but only partly. It was a beautiful sentiment, but it reminded her how alone she always felt. She wondered what it would be like to have someone by your side—friend or spouse—to help you and encourage your dreams.

A ball of energy came bounding down the stairs, interrupting their musings.

"There you are!" Morgan said breathlessly. "I've been waiting to show you your room! Come on!" She reached past her mother and grabbed Aster's hand, pulling her up the stairs.

"Morgan! Be gentle with our guest, please!" Flora yelled after them. "Aster, if you're hungry, just come down to the kitchen, and I'll fix you something," she added, letting Morgan take over as tour guide.

Morgan led Aster past a couple of floors with rooms and then passed through a small doorway entering the tree itself.

How high are we going to go? Aster wondered.

"Almost there!" Morgan said.

Her quick reply made Aster feel once again like the little girl could read her thoughts, but she told herself it was just her paranoia.

Aster lost count of how many floors they passed as they wound up the tree. The smell of wood permeated her nose and made her think of the times her father had built things for the house or made repairs. She had always loved that smell.

Morgan eventually stopped at a small hallway with two doors facing each other.

"Ta-da!" Morgan declared. "I told you it was the best room in the inn," she said, spreading her arms out wide to display the room for Aster.

Aster, still trying to catch her breath, let out a little gasp.

Pale-blue walls gave the room a calming feeling looking almost white with the amount of light streaming in from the balcony doors. Double-glass doors sent rays of light sparkling into the room, creating little rainbows.

The carvings around the room sent a jolt through her system. The four-poster bed had detailed carvings of vines and flowers on each post.

Not just any flower, though.

Collin had clearly carved an aster flower into the wood.

The same flower that served as her namesake. Her mother had always loved asters, and Mother planted them all over their garden back home. She had named Aster after them because of this.

The next surprise came when she'd noticed the top of the headboard had a flower crown composed of none other than aster blooms. They looked so real Aster had to remind herself it was just wood carvings.

The minute they entered the town, she felt something similar to what she felt in Mag's clearing. She couldn't quite name it, and the thought that came to mind made her feel silly for even considering.

It felt like magic. A wonderful magic that filled her with awe and wonder, and even, dare she say it— hope.

"Do you like it?" Morgan finally asked.

"Oh, yes!" Aster replied quickly. "I haven't seen the other rooms, but I can imagine that this truly is the best one." She walked around the room, feeling the soft jade quilt on the bed, which she noticed had been hand-stitched with little white asters.

Morgan opened the balcony doors and motioned for her. "Come, look at the view!"

Aster followed the eager little girl out onto the balcony, her mouth dropping in wonder.

She knew the city was beautiful, but this gave her a whole new view.

Below them, the garden spread out like a tablecloth covering the earth. Flora had planted a wide range of flowers that created a beautiful tapestry to view from above. From her balcony, Aster could see bright-yellow buttercups, red campion, and stark-white wild carrots.

It didn't surprise Aster to find they were on the top floor. She looked out on the tightly-knit city, with so many levels she lost count. She imagined what her sister would think if she could see it all.

"There's my brother!" Morgan said, startling Aster.

She followed Morgan's pointing finger to a little boy running through the garden towards Collin and Josiah. Collin swept the little boy up, spinning him around in a circle. She watched as he introduced him to Josiah, who tousled the little boy's hair and interacted with him in a way that made Aster grin.

Perhaps you're not completely against this type of life, she thought to herself smugly.

"What type of life is Josiah against?" Morgan asked curiously.

Aster turned her head so quickly she thought her neck might snap. Once again, Morgan had showed she could hear Aster's thoughts.

What was this child?

Could she be a young mind searcher?

The carved aster flowers, the empty inn, and the convenience of Josiah's friend being the innkeeper began to all cumulate together, heightening Aster's suspicions.

"Morgan," Aster asked through the barrage of panic, "why did you just ask me that?"

Morgan shrugged, but Aster wasn't about to let it go.

"And earlier, when I was thinking how much longer till we reached my room?"

Morgan shrugged and avoided looking Aster in the face.

Aster continued to press her.

"When we first met, you greeted us out of the blue, right when I was wondering where Josiah and I would stay."

Morgan ignored Aster's question and went back inside. Aster followed her, not giving up on this idea that somehow Morgan and her family held a connection to the Light Keepers.

"Morgan, wait, please, I think you can hear my thoughts, and I just—"

"Please don't ask me again!" Morgan cried out, whirling around, revealing her eyes brimming with tears.

Aster's heart wrenched at the sight, and her stomach clenched with guilt. In her curiosity and desire to solve this mystery, she had made a little girl cry.

"Morgan, Morgan," Aster soothed, kneeling, so she was level with the sad little girl. "I'm sorry. I forgot my manners, and I pushed you for answers on something you know nothing about. I'm so sorry, just forget I asked. Okay? I guess I'm more tired than I realized, and I wasn't thinking." Morgan wiped her eyes and shook her head.

"But you were thinking," she mumbled.

Aster leaned back and stared at her, "Morgan, what…"

Flora interrupted them, coming through the door. "Morgan, let Aster—" The words died on her lips when she saw Aster and her teary-eyed daughter. "What on earth?" she asked, stunned.

"Momma, I didn't mean to, I promise!" Morgan rushed to Flora and buried her face in her skirt. "I didn't say anything when she asked. I promise I didn't!"

"Sh, sh," Flora said, stroking her daughter's hair to soothe and calm her down. "It's okay, darling, I know you didn't. Sh, shh." She lifted the girl up and held her close, giving her a big hug to show everything was going to be okay. "Now, no more tears."

Flora set Morgan down and tilted her chin up. "I want you to go downstairs and help set the table for dinner. Then go outside and play, and I'll call you in when it's time."

She gave Morgan another hug and shooed her off. Morgan ran out of the room.

Flora shut the door and paused. Aster gulped and stood up, feeling awful at having pushed Morgan to tears. She was sure Flora was about to give her a well-deserved tongue-lashing.

"I'm sorry about that," Flora said, turning around to face her.

Aster's eyes widened; she had not expected an apology.

Flora motioned for her to sit down on the bed, and joined her, sighing as she did.

"I knew I should have followed you all up here, instead of

letting Morgan be alone with you. She doesn't quite know how to ignore what she hears, and so she answers people's thoughts without thinking. It's hard to teach a little girl, even one as bright as Morgan, to know the difference between someone speaking out loud and just thinking to themselves."

Aster was trying to get used to Flora's quick talking patterns, but she felt overwhelmed with more questions. Flora seemed to sense this and laughed.

"Collin says I need to work on the speed with which I speak, especially when I'm attempting to explain something important." She took a deep breath. "Let me start again. I'm sure you've already guessed by now, but Morgan is a mind searcher. Of course, it's too early to know if it will become more than extreme intuition." Flora paused, and Aster spoke up.

"Are you and Collin mind searchers'?" she asked.

Flora nodded. "Yes, and no. Collin is, though he doesn't practice it anymore, and it's been so long I'm not sure he could anymore if he tried. My parents and his are also mind searchers, I was born without the ability. We weren't sure what our children would have when they were born, but it was obvious—as Morgan's ability has recently showed itself. However, our other two seem to have taken after me."

This new world Aster had entered became increasingly interesting to her. She tried to take it all in. She was learning more and more with every step of their journey.

"Collin is one of the Light Keepers that Josiah helped protect?"

Flora smiled and nodded. "Yes, and he saved his life once. If it weren't for Josiah, Collin and I wouldn't have gotten married. I think his near-death experience made him reevaluate his life, which is when we met. When he heard Josiah was coming, Collin acted like a kid on their birthday."

"How did he know, though?" Aster asked, becoming less surprised by these twists the more they appeared.

Before Flora could answer, Aster knew.

"Mag," she stated matter-of-factly.

"Yes, Mag didn't wait long after you all left to send us word, we might receive visitors soon. She said we needed to be prepared for them if they should arrive."

The problem happened, though, when Morgan heard about the news. She has stayed on high alert since, because she was excited to meet another mind searcher who's a girl. I think when you got closer to Cedrus, she could sense you, or hear your thoughts. I'm not sure which. All I know is one minute today she's helping me in the kitchen, and the next she drops the eggs, shells and all, and runs out of the house saying, They're here!"

Aster just shook her head. "I thought we were on our own when we lost Andi and Roark. I couldn't imagine Josiah and I making it through this without help." She grabbed Flora's hand and gave it a squeeze. "I'm so glad Morgan heard us coming."

Flora squeezed her hand back and smiled. "I am, too. But tell me," Flora said, "what happened to Andi and Roark? Are they okay? Collin and I have known them for ages, and Andi was always so kind to me, despite my lack of ability."

"That sounds like her," Aster said, smiling.

"How did you all become separated?" Flora asked in almost a whisper, concerned by Aster's answer.

Aster sighed. "I had an episode at the edge of the woods, before we made it to the main road leading to Venari. I still don't know how to control my ability. It just happened, and a group of Cu-Sith discovered us almost immediately."

She didn't feel like mentioning her and Josiah's theory that they were something much more dangerous than Cu-Sith.

Flora gasped. "How did you get away?"

"I kept their leader talking," Aster continued, shuddering at the memory, "and Roark broke free, began fighting him. Andi tried fighting a few as well. I was a big help by fainting," she added. "Josiah had to sweep me up on the horse and ride off." She kept out the part about the one Cu-Sith grabbing her ankle. Just the mere thought of it made her sick to her stomach.

Flora lowered her hand from her mouth, but evidently the story of their harrowing circumstance had shaken her. "And Andi and Roark?" she asked, fearing the worst.

"We're not sure," Aster whispered, her eyes watering.

The guilt filled her for leaving them behind, but she knew Josiah had done the right thing. She also knew Roark and Andi were strong, and if anyone could get free of the Cu-Sith, it was them, especially working together.

Flora remained silent for a moment, taking in the news her friends may be in dire trouble, or worse. "I'm sure they're fine," she said.

Aster wondered if she was trying to convince Aster or herself. Either way, Aster gave her hand a comforting squeeze. They gave each other a half smile.

"You did the right thing," Flora added.

Aster could tell she was sincere, but the guilt still nudged her.

"I just hope we made the right decision taking this route. It's not that I think you all can't be of help to us!" She didn't want to give Flora the wrong impression. "I'm just concerned that if Andi and Roark got free, then they're going to follow our original route, and they may take time looking for us."

Flora nodded. "It's all right, I understand what you mean. However, I think Josiah was right to bring you here. I'm surprised Roark wanted to take the route through Venari. It's not safe for regular people, let alone Light Keepers."

"Josiah thought it was strange as well, but he couldn't persuade Roark to change his mind."

"I know why he wanted to travel through Venari." Josiah leaned against the doorway, startling them both.

"Come on, I'll tell you about it all downstairs with Collin." He turned on his heels and headed back down the stairs.

Flora looked perplexed. Aster was frustrated, feeling like everyone, she'd put her trust in had done nothing but keep secrets from her.

A moment later, they followed Josiah down the stairs, stopped at the bottom by two identical, small redheaded children.

"That red whirlwind would be our twins, Sean and Erin," Flora laughed, catching Aster's surprised reaction.

They joined Josiah and Collin in the kitchen, located behind a hidden door in the parlor. A wonderful smell of freshly baked bread and cinnamon greeted them as they entered. There was a giant stone oven on one wall, a large table covered in flour and baking ingredients in the middle of the floor, and off to the right, a beautiful alcove made up of glass windows. Light poured inside and cast shadows around the room.

Flora noticed Aster taking it all in and smiled. "Collin fixed up the kitchen before anything else. He added the sunroom, moved the flowers to the other end of the garden, and planted an herb garden outside the door." She pointed to the kitchen door, located at the back of the kitchen.

"Oh, and of course that giant stone monster," she said, pointing toward the stone oven.

"Don't let her fool you," Collin said from the sunroom, where he and Josiah sat waiting. "She knows that oven and what I make of it. If it weren't for that oven, we would have starved."

Aster saw Flora roll her eyes at her husband's dramatic explanation.

"Well, what is it you all discovered?" Flora asked, ignoring his comment. "Why did Roark choose the Venari route?"

"Josiah told me about his disagreement with Roark," Collin began. "It made little sense to me, either, but Roark and I have often been on opposite sides of opinions. Then I remembered a letter I received about a month ago from Roark himself. I had forgotten about it until Josiah told me about Roark's determination to travel through Venari. Even though Cedrus is the clearly safer and quicker route."

"And?" Flora prompted.

"I'm getting there, darling," Collin replied with a smirk.

"Get there quicker, dear," Flora volleyed back.

Josiah sighed.

Collin cleared his throat. "Thankfully, I still have the letter." And with a flourish, he took it out of his front jacket pocket and read,

> "*C,*
>
> *I hope you are well and that you are taking care of your flowers. I would come and visit you all, but I've heard one of your rooms has wood rot. I don't feel comfortable staying in such a place, especially since you don't know which room is the infected party. I'll stick with the new place. At least I know which rooms to avoid there. Watch out before the*

rot gets closer to your own room. I worry about you and your flowers.
Your friend,
R"

"What on earth?" Flora asked in surprise. "We don't have wood rot in the inn! Why would he write such a thing?"

"Of course, we don't have rot," Collin replied defensively. "That's why I chalked the letter up to nonsense. But now, I'm thinking there's something to it. I think it's a.-"

"Code," Aster interrupted without meaning to. "I'm sorry!" she amended quickly.

To her frustration, out of the corner of her eye, she saw Josiah smirk.

"No, no, it's okay. Just take away from my shocking revelation," Collin sighed, feigning offense. "You're right, though, it's some type of code. I think by flowers he means Flora and the children, and by rooms he means.-"

"That someone in Cedrus is a spy," Aster interrupted again, without apologizing this time. "That someone here is a spy, and we can't trust them. Either one of the Evanders' lackeys or someone worse." Her voice trailed off when she realized she had completely taken over Collin's code-breaking.

Collin humphed.

Flora laughed and elbowed him jokingly. "See, dear, that's how you tell an important story, straight to the point."

Collin rolled his eyes and shrugged. "Well, I would've given more background, but I guess your way works, too, fellow mind searcher," he added with a smirk.

Josiah's head snapped up, and he glared at Collin. Collin threw his hands up in defense.

"Josiah?" Aster asked, surprised by his reaction towards his friend. She didn't mind he called her a Light Keeper, even if she hadn't gotten used to her new identity yet.

"I'm sorry," Collin said, looking at Josiah. "I forgot your theory on the matter."

"What theory?" Aster asked, confused.

Josiah sighed, crossing his arms in a huff. "I think it's safest if we mention nothing about who we are. Especially you. Especially out loud. Someone could be walking by or hiding outside and overhear us. Or the children might repeat it without knowing what they're saying."

Flora grabbed Collin's arm and looked at him with budding fear. "Collin, do you think we're in danger, too?"

He put a reassuring hand over his wife's and stared at her straight on. "No, no. I think we're fine right now. That letter came almost two months ago, and we have seen nothing suspicious."

Flora took a deep breath and released her grip, turning her eyes on Josiah. "They won't say anythin. Our children know better," she said with an air of a mama bear protecting her cubs. "The twins move too fast to hear a word we say. Morgan knows the rules. She wouldn't say anything." She paused when she mentioned Morgan.

Flora and Aster shared a glance.

Josiah and Collin caught their shared look, though, and didn't like it.

"What is it?" they said in tandem.

Aster watched Flora's eyes widen in fear. Flora turned swiftly and walked out of the kitchen.

"Flora!" Collin asked in shock. "Where are you going?"

"We have to find Morgan!" she called back.

Josiah and Collin looked at Aster, as they all followed immediately after Flora.

"We had a bit of drama earlier while you all were having revelations," Aster tried explaining.

"What kind of drama?" Josiah asked.

"Morgan's powers have recently been more attuned, and more so since you and Aster came into town," Flora said as they caught up to her, continuing to search for Morgan.

"Morgan kept replying to my thoughts," Aster continued, trying to keep up with the others. "I thought it was just a coincidence at first, but I started asking her a lot of questions. She became upset, but she stayed strong and kept her silence on the matter."

Flora searched the dining room, then headed for the parlor, desperately glancing around.

"Morgan!" she called out, trying to sound calm.

Collin caught Flora by the shoulders and gazed into her eyes. "Flora, what's wrong?"

Her eyes kept darting around. "It's fine. I took care of it. After what you discovered, I think we need to keep Morgan in the house." She looked up into his face, fear and concern clouding her eyes. "If someone is out there and Morgan reads their thoughts and accidentally gives them any sign of it, like she did with Aster, then we might have trouble."

Collin processed this new information, nodded, and let go of Flora.

"Morgan!" he yelled.

They all began searching, calling out for the little girl.

"Morgan?"

"Morgan, where are you?"

"Sean, Erin," Collin asked the twins, who were playing by the steps, "have you seen your sister?"

"No", they replied in unison, going about their business, too busy with playing to sense the grown-ups' distress.

Aster had a sudden thought as they searched desperately for the little girl.

She'd read something in her great-grandmother's journal mentioning mind searchers communicating telepathically with each other. She couldn't quite remember how, but she knew to read anyone else's thoughts, she had to be looking at them.

Perhaps if I picture Morgan, I can create the same effect as before.

She closed her eyes and stood still, ignoring Josiah's voice, asking her what she was doing. Instead, she focused wholly on Morgan, what she looked like, their interactions so far, and the girl's sweet demeanor.

She felt warmth at her fingertips, as if they were hovering over a candle flame.

Morgan, where are you? Aster thought hard.

Silence.

She tried again. The warmth surged up her arms, but this time she didn't feel engulfed by it; instead it felt like a comforting blanket keeping away the chill of winter.

Morgan, we're all worried. We can't find you.

Still nothing.

Morgan, please. She thought harder.

Aster?

Aster's eyes flew open at the sound of Morgan's voice in her head, almost losing the connection.

She took a deep breath and refocused.

Morgan! Where are you? Are you okay?

I'm fine! I'm in the garden. I went to find flowers for your room, but I saw some beyond the yard that looked better.

Aster almost shrieked. She suddenly saw Morgan's location. It was a faint picture, like trying to read in the dark. She could barely see the outline of the inn.

I see! Aster replied. *Stay there! We're coming!*

She opened her eyes and jumped back when she saw everyone staring at her in shock. The fire receded from her body, sending a chill through her.

Shivering, she addressed Flora's and Collin's worried looks. "Morgan's fine, she's in the garden out back."

Without asking how she knew, Flora and Collin ran outside to the gardens. Aster felt her feet glued to the floor. Her theory had worked, and reading the journal had come in handy.

"Are you okay?" Josiah asked softly, putting his hand on her chilled arm.

She nodded. "I think."

They stood there for another minute before Collin, and Flora came back in, Morgan between them.

"Thank you, Aster," Flora said, her voice shaking.

"I got flowers for your room!" Morgan said, holding out the bouquet of wild carrots and buttercups.

"Morgan knows she's not allowed to go out again without telling us first. Right, Morgan?" Collin said with mock seriousness—that was only somewhat mocking. The situation obviously shook him.

"Aster found me, though, Papa," Morgan said.

Aster's heart rate was just returning to normal.

She swallowed hard. "Morgan, your papa is right."

However, now that Morgan was safely in her parents' arms, Aster was glad for the real-life exercise of her ability. She still couldn't believe her idea had worked. How much did her powers do, precisely? She was realizing why Mag had wanted them to reach the Academy as quickly as possible.

Morgan released her father and looked up at Aster with her enormous eyes. She motioned for Aster to lean in so she could whisper something in her ear.

Aster didn't hesitate and leaned down to the little girl.

"I've never met another girl like me before," she whispered.

Aster's heart clenched at the joy and sadness mixed in the little girl's words. She knew what it was like to be different from your friends and family. Her parents knew she had been a mind searcher, but they had kept the truth from her and tried to diminish her powers. She wished she had had parents like Flora and Collin, though even they encouraged their daughter to hide her ability to an extent.

Aster wondered how many other little girls were like her and Morgan, growing up feeling like they didn't belong, no one willing to understand them.

Aster wrapped Morgan in a hug—the hug of two outcasts feeling like someone understood them, understood what it was like to be different.

Thank you.

You're welcome.

Chapter 10

We have to leave," Josiah declared later, after Collin and Flora sent Morgan up to her room to play.

The four of them sat in the sun room, replaying the last fifteen minutes in their heads.

"What do you mean you have to leave?" Flora asked. "You just got here and haven't rested or gathered up supplies."

Aster wanted to add that they were safer here as well, but Roark's coded warning rang through her thoughts. She didn't want to leave Cedrus, especially not Flora and Collin and their little family. But the unknown spy Roark mentioned posed a danger not only for her and Josiah but for Flora and Collin as well.

"Josiah's right," she relented. "We can't stay here if there's someone looking for us. It might just be one of the Evanders' guards, but it could be worse."

Josiah nodded. "Precisely. We'll gather up necessary supplies, but then we need to take your boat and get down-river as soon as possible."

Collin nodded in reluctant agreement, but Flora still protested. "No, Collin, tell Josiah he's wrong."

"Flora," Collin said, "he's right. They need to leave as soon as possible. However—"

Flora looked hopeful, and Josiah tried to interrupt before Collin held up his hand.

"Listen, Josiah, I agree with you, but I also know that everyone saw you all come through here. If there's a spy here, waiting for you, they knew the minute you entered the city. What I propose is that you stay till dark, then take the boat down river. Create a show of staying so the person thinks they have time to catch you. When it's dark, we'll sneak out the back to the river. By morning, if they come looking, it will seem like you vanished.

That will give you plenty of a head start."

Aster watched as Josiah crossed his arms and pulled his head in like a turtle. She was learning this was Josiah's thinking posture. His head went deeper into his shoulders depending on the level of importance of the decision. This time it was farther in than she had ever seen it.

He sighed and poked his head back out of his shell. "You're right, and that's a good idea," he said with great reluctance.

"Ha!" Collin laughed and gave him a brotherly slap on the back. "My favorite thing to hear! Flora, remember that phrase for the many times you'll need it in the future."

Flora rolled her eyes and put her attention on Aster. "Let's get you packed, and then we'll pick something out for you to wear this evening."

"I can just wear what I've been wearing to travel," Aster said.

Flora laughed. "Oh no, I don't mean for traveling, I mean for the Vesta."

"No, we can't go to the Vesta," Josiah protested. "We don't want to be that obvious."

"Yes, my friend, you do," Collin replied. "People need to see you as late as possible, so whoever the 'rot' is doesn't think you're trying to escape. They'll never think you'd leave after dark, so they'll wait till tomorrow to come after you."

"What is the Vesta?" Aster asked. She felt so uninformed.

Floral groaned. "I'm sorry, of course you wouldn't know. This is still new for you. Here in Cedrus, we still believe in the Light Keepers and an united Ignis. Many in Cedrus were born to Light Keepers yet have no ability, like me. Like-minded believers meet at the Vesta to pray and tell stories."

"I still think that makes us too exposed," Josiah grumbled.

Aster shook her head in disagreement. "I think they're right, plus I need to learn more about Light Keepers and all that entails. This sounds like a perfect opportunity."

"Fine," Josiah said reluctantly, getting up from his chair and stomping out of the room.

Aster watched him walk away. She was becoming progressively frustrated with Josiah's attitude since they had arrived in Cedrus. She thought finding Collin and Flora would have been encouraging to him. It had lifted her spirits. However, she could sense the guilt for leaving Roark and Andi still clinging to him.

"He feels bad for leaving Roark and Andi behind," Aster said to Collin and Flora.

"Yes," Collin said, following her gaze. "He needs to move on and concentrate on the task at hand."

"He will," Aster said.

She could feel Collin's inquisitive gaze on her, and she realized she was still staring after Josiah.

"Flora, you said we could pack a few supplies, right?" Aster said, attempting to divert Collin's attention.

"Yes, let's prepare the bags, then we can focus on what you'll wear to Vesta."

Flora linked her arm in Aster's and led her back up to the house.

"Don't worry," she whispered, "your secret is safe with me." She winked.

Aster felt her face flush, and she ignored the comment. She didn't know what secret Flora was alluding to—at least, she didn't want to admit it.

Flora grabbed a couple rucksacks from a hook by the door of the large kitchen, and with Aster's help, filled them with basic supplies she and Josiah would need on their journey. The children thundered down the stairs as Collin fixed dinner.

Aster and Flora took a break to eat with the others, with Josiah noticeably absent. Aster felt bad for him; he couldn't even allow himself a few moments to enjoy being with his good friend, but she remembered her mother once saying that everyone deals with their feelings differently, and you had to respect how they dealt with them if it wasn't harmful to themselves or others.

She allowed herself to enjoy the family atmosphere.

It was her first slice of normality since Andi and Roark had whisked her away on this journey. The children's conversations, laughter, and the feeling of love all around the table gave her more fortification for whatever lay ahead than any nap would do at this point.

"You'll love the Vesta time!" Morgan said between mouthfuls as they discussed the evening ahead.

"I'm looking forward to it. The Vesta sounds similar to the chapels around Veridi," she commented. "We had one in the town near my home, but my parents didn't take us there often."

"Good for them," Collin said.

Aster looked at him.

"Well," he explained, "the Evanders created chapels as a compromise with the Light Keepers and those who continued to believe in the King after Ignis split. The Light Keepers wanted to continue with their traditions, including the Vestas the King had created, but the Evanders feared this would keep the story of Ignis too real. They believed the Vestas kept the King and the idea of a united Ignis alive. They wanted to reduce it to a legend. So, they created chapels, and the Light Keepers, who wanted to maintain a peaceful relationship tried these, but they soon saw them for what they were—a diversion. The Evanders dressed the buildings up, making them pretty and appealing, but they taught nothing of substance within the walls. Your parents were wise to keep you from it."

Aster felt stunned by this alternative history, yet it made perfect sense. The Evanders realized if they ever wanted full control of Ignis, the fighting had to stop. They'd created fake compromises with those of the original, united Ignis.

"The Evanders have tried wiping out Light Keepers, but you all have survived here," Aster observed.

"Being so close to the Green River has its perks," Collin answered mischievously. "They haven't tried to stop us because of the 'legends' surrounding these woods, and especially the Green River. Storms keep occurring and taking away more land around us, and the Evanders have been doing their best to cut us off, to force us out. They won't stop till.-"

"Collin," Flora interrupted. "Little ears."

Aster glanced at the children, having forgotten for a moment they were there. She felt awful for bringing up the topic in front of them, but she was desperate to understand.

"Yes, dear," Collin said, returning to his food.

Aster finished the rest of her lunch in silence, contemplating all Collin had said. She glanced at Josiah's full plate and empty chair.

"I'll be right back." She pushed back from the table and picked up his plate.

"Aster..." Collin started, but Flora nudged him and gave him a look.

"What?" he asked, confused.

Flora replied, "The room across the hall from yours."

Aster smiled, took the full plate, and began the trek upstairs.

She located Josiah's room across the hall from hers, just as Flora had told her.

No coincidence, she thought.

She gently knocked on the door carved with a beautiful stag. No answer.

She knocked again.

No answer.

She knocked again and tried the doorknob, which was unlocked. Entering the room, she was surprised to find it empty. Josiah also had a small balcony, but he wasn't on there, either.

"Where are you, Josiah?" she muttered under her breath, becoming concerned she couldn't find him.

"Look up," said a voice from above.

"Ah!" Aster screamed. Her hands shot up, sending Josiah's food flying off the balcony and down, down, down to the ground below.

Laughter erupted above her, and she took a step back to look up, only to find Josiah sitting on a large branch above the balcony, his legs curled up, and doubled over with laughter.

She put her hands on her hips and frowned up at him. "Josiah! What are you doing up there? Aren't we high up enough already? Why would you sit up there? There's a perfectly good balcony, with a railing! Why aren't you downstairs with the rest of us? We had a wonderfully good time, and you've missed out on it."

She took a deep breath, feeling like Flora's fast talking must be contagious, when Josiah stopped laughing and carefully jumped down, swinging off the branch and plopping onto the balcony.

He was still grinning as he looked over the railing.

"Was that my lunch?" he asked, pointing to the broken plate and pieces of food scattered in the yard.

She shoved him. "Yes. That's what you deserve for acting like this."

He said nothing, just leaned his elbows on the balcony, propping his head in his hands.

Aster didn't want to push him to talk, but she also knew this holding it in wasn't doing him any good, either.

He broke the silence.

"I should have gone back for them."

"Josiah, no," Aster moaned. "You know Roark wouldn't have wanted you to feel guilty. Plus, if you had gone back, they would have taken you, and I'd be on my own."

Silence again, so Aster continued, "I feel guilty, too, you know." She joined him, leaning against the balcony, and staring down at the ground, where some grateful animals were enjoying Josiah's lunch.

He looked at her, surprised by her statement, but she ignored it and played the silent card back to him.

"Why do you feel guilty?" he asked.

"Because this is all my fault. We're on the run because of me. The Cu-Sith, or whatever they were, came after me. We wouldn't have lost Andi and Roark if I had let them take me."

"Aster, stop, of course you weren't going to go with them." He roughly shoved his hand through his hair. "This isn't your fault, it's not Roark's or Andis... and... I suppose, you're right—it's not mine either."

She gave him a raised eyebrow in return.

"It happened this way for a reason. If Roark had told you sooner, we might be in the same boat," he continued.

"Thanks for that," Aster whispered. "Here I came to encourage you, and you just encouraged both of us."

He scoffed and pushed back from the balcony, giving her a shrewd look. "That's some good mental manipulation there, mind princess."

She blanched. "Ugh, what an awful nickname!"

"Hey, I think it's a great nickname," he in with mock

defense.

"We can't be certain I'm one of the three from the prophecy," she said, crossing her arms to ward off the slight chill in the breeze.

"Aster, please," Josiah said. "Didn't your interactions with Morgan give you enough proof?"

"No," she replied doggedly. "It proves a little girl has the same power as me."

Josiah gave her a scorching look, but she turned away, ignoring him. She admitted her abilities were real, but perhaps they were nothing more than that of a regular mind searcher. They needed her to do something she wasn't sure she believed she could.

"Aster, you can't deny who you are. If you do, it will only dampen your ability, and then you won't just be harming yourself but everyone who needs you," Josiah said with conviction.

She saw the passion on his face. "What do you mean I'll be harming others?"

He sighed and ran his hands through his hair. "Aster, I don't think you realize…"

He stopped himself, but she instantly sensed there was something important he was keeping from her. "Josiah, what aren't you telling me? I'm not the only Light Keeper. Isn't there another Light Keeper with the same power who can help you?"

He just looked at her, and she could sense emotions of sadness and confusion mixing through his thoughts.

"You don't get it, do you?" he whispered.

"Get what?"

"If we don't find the Knight soon, they'll wipe us out."

Aster felt a prick of fear flow through her. "Aren't there enough Light Keepers to overtake the Evanders?" she asked, realizing how naïve she must sound.

Josiah sighed and sat down in one of the balcony chairs. "Believe it or not, the Evanders aren't our biggest problem."

"What's worse than the Evanders hiring Cu-Sith to take me out?" Aster asked, the prick of fear spreading.

"There's a man named Malum," Josiah said. "He leads a

group that call themselves the Kasmiens. Their goal is to force people to forget about Light Keepers and a united Ignis to ultimately wipe us out—along with anyone who believes in us. They don't care about Ignis, they only care about killing all who might remain loyal to the King and the Knight. They believe their purpose is to reorder the world in their own way."

"Why didn't Roark or Andi tell me about this?" she asked.

"There isn't enough proof Malum or his followers are in Venari. Plus, many believe they aren't real."

"Why?" Aster asked in a terrified whisper.

"Because they…they're described as shape-shifters… monsters. We can't get the survivors to provide us with descriptions of the Kasmiens because they're so afraid. The Evanders chalk up their attacks as being done by the Cu-Sith. We've discovered most of those attacked have been Light Keepers or have ties to them. But I overheard mention of them in the market the other day as I was leaving the town to go warn your family, the day we ran."

Aster felt overwhelmed by this news, but she didn't want Josiah to see her fear. Instead, she took a deep breath and straightened her shoulders.

"Okay, so that's most likely who's after us. You think that this group, the Kasmiens, and their leader, Malum, are the ones who attacked the school," she stated matter-of-factly, pacing the room as she listed off the obvious. "Most likely one of them was sent here in case we came this route. Which is what Roark was referring to in his coded letter to Collin. We must get to the Academy as soon as possible."

She was stating the obvious, but it helped her see where everything lay Aster handled situations better when she could organize her thoughts.

Josiah just nodded, letting her go through her process.

"Now I understand why you wanted to leave right away," she said, hating to admit he was right.

"Yes, but Collin is right, too. It would be safer to make our presence known, since it already is, and make it seem like we're staying overnight. I do hate the danger it could put Collin and his family in, but they know the risks. Plus, it will be nice to go to the Vesta."

She grasped on to this new topic. "You've been to a Vesta before?"

"Yes," he replied, and she noticed a peaceful look fill his face. "On top of it being a beautiful building, it's a wonderful experience as well. It will be good for both of us, especially you."

"Why me?" she asked, surprised.

"You'll see," he said.

She glared at him, hating the added mystery to the situation.

Before she could ask a follow-up question, he went back into his room. She realized he would not give her any more information.

"You should go get ready," he said.

"Where are you going?" she asked.

He smirked. "I'm going to ask Collin to fix me another plate, since someone threw mine off the balcony."

Chapter 11

Aster's mind swirled with thoughts of Josiah's comment about how going to the Vesta would help her.

How?

Why?

"There you are," Flora said when Aster returned to her room across the hall.

"Yes, sorry, I forgot about getting ready," Aster replied, sitting down on the bed in a daze.

"Is everything all right?" Flora asked as she laid what looked like art supplies on the vanity. "I thought I heard you scream from across the hall."

Aster laughed. "Oh, that, Josiah just scared me half to death is all. I'm fine."

Flora gave her a look.

"Truly, I am," Aster insisted, hoping she sounded more convincing the second time. She tried changing the subject by asking about the items Flora had set out on the vanity. "What is all this?" She picked up a jar of green powder and noticed a basket of various leaves and a few paint brushes laid out ready to use.

"Oh, these are to help you blend in a little."

"I thought the whole point was for us to stand out?" Aster asked, lifting a palm frond out of the basket.

"Yes, but we can't have you being a distraction. In Cedrus, we hold this time in great regard. You're an outsider already. If you arrive looking like one, you'll be a distraction."

"Ah," Aster said, realizing that her extensive reading couldn't have prepared her enough to deal with meeting new people in a strange place.

"I've only ever lived on the outskirts of town. We went into town for school and market days. We mingled little with those behind the town walls. The one time I asked my parents why, my mother told me they didn't want us polluted with all the goings-on. But now I just wonder if it was to keep me away from people because they worried someone might recognize my powers."

"I'm sure they wanted the best for you. Even if they went about it the wrong way," Flora remarked thoughtfully.

"Maybe…" Aster mused. "I just hope I get to see them again so I can ask them why they kept so many secrets."

"You'll see them again," Flora encouraged. "Just have faith."

Aster offered her a slight smile, but she was so tired and worn out, she didn't know if she had the strength to grab hold of any faith.

Flora sat her down in front of the mirror. Aster grimaced at her reflection. She hadn't realized how bad she looked, from the attack in the clearing and then traveling nonstop to Cedrus.

"I look awful," Aster said, fiddling with her hair, which stuck up at various unpleasant angles. "You have your work cut out for you."

Flora scoffed. "Oh, stop it. After all you've been through, you look fine." Aster made her a face that said she didn't believe her, but she didn't push the subject.

Flora flew to work, focusing on her task, moving so swiftly Aster could scarcely tell what she was doing. She took the green powder, which Aster assumed was the chlorophyll powder Josiah had mentioned when they arrived.

"I've read so many books about Veridi that mention Cedrus as a city of trees," Aster commented as Flora worked, "but none of them have ever mentioned customs or anything specific about the culture here."

"That's another way the Evanders try to make us a legend, like the Knight and a united Ignis," Flora replied, with sadness and a tinge of anger in her tone.

"I'm so sorry..." Aster whispered. She didn't know what else to say to someone forced out of their home, for the simple reason, that her people believed something different. Aster was realizing her books hadn't prepared her for everything. Perhaps she was naïve, or she desperately wanted to believe in a fair world. The town of had Verd never treated her family as bad as the Evanders treated the people of Cedrus.

"It's all right. I'm glad Roark and Andi found you," Flora said with a glimmer of light in her eyes. "It gives me hope my children might see the rebirth of Ignis, as it should have always been. You do not know how much happier Collin and I have been since Mag sent word about your potential arrival."

Aster swallowed hard.

Her stomach tied itself in knots as the pressure and expectation on her shoulders grew heavier. Flora's hope didn't reassure her of the purpose being thrust on her. Instead, it gave her more proof; she couldn't be one of the keys to saving Ignis. Yes, she'd experienced an episode with Mag and the Knight's letter, but maybe it was just her ability as a Light Keeper.

Maybe I'm simply the key to finding *the Flower with a Royal Mind*, she thought to herself.

She stayed silent, weighing everything she was continuing to learn about the Knight and the truth of Ignis's past and future.

Flora used a wet brush to blend the green powders on her face and down her arms, creating the camouflage look Aster noticed on the citizens of Cedrus when she'd first arrived.

Flora sprinkled some of the remaining powder in her hair, which she had brushed through and braided, allowing a few strands to fall naturally on the sides of her face. She also intertwined a few leaves through the braids, which Aster thought created a fantastic, finished look.

After she finished, Flora showed Aster the dress she had hung up for her to wear. "It's one of my old ones, but it should fit you. I can always pin it up for a quick fix if needed."

Aster took the dress, feeling the soft linen between her fingers. Her family couldn't always afford such delicate fabrics, which normally meant wearing itchy clothing. This dress, though, was soft yet had a strange texture on the outside that Aster couldn't quite place.

"It's made to mimic the feel of bark on a tree," Flora said, noticing Aster's quizzical expression.

"It's wonderful," Aster said, watching the wind from the open doors blow the dress, creating a beautiful effect. "Ooh!"

Aster gasped.

When the sleeves fluttered in the wind, it showed off various hues of green, revealing a hidden pattern of leaves.

Flora laughed and smiled, proud of the reaction the dress elicited from Aster.

"The sleeves are my favorite part, too," she said, holding the sleeve out to catch the sun from the window.

Aster received another shock as the sun streamed through the sleeves and cast shadows on the opposite wall. The shadows resembled leaves as well.

"Thank you, Flora," Aster said. She was rendered nearly speechless by the beautiful dress.

"It's the least I can do for you," Flora replied, causing the sinking feeling in Aster to return. Nothing could take away the truth, not even a beautiful dress or braided hair. Countless lives and hopes rested on her.

The setting sun streamed in through the glass doors as Aster finished prepping for their visit to the Vesta. She stepped outside on the balcony and took a deep breath, catching whiffs of dinners being prepared and the comforting smells of the woods surrounding her.

She had the distinct feeling of being watched. Whipping around, she saw it was only Josiah. He was leaning against the doorway, staring at her with a funny look she couldn't quite decipher. He stood straight when he realized she'd noticed him.

"Sorry, I didn't mean to startle you, I just... I…"

She tried not to laugh as he struggled to get words to form.

He took a deep breath and started again. "Flora told me to come get you so we can leave for the Vesta." He paused, as if considering his next words. "You look nice."

He said it so hastily Aster almost didn't catch what he said, but his blush confirmed it.

"Thank you," she replied. "You clean up nicely,too" She regarded his outfit, evidently supplied by Collin, of dark-brown trousers, and a light-green vest, tied with a darker green belt made of the same material as her sleeves.

He blushed again and held out his hand for her.

She took it and let him lead her down the stairs and outside, where the others were waiting.

Morgan ran up to Aster and pulled her along the path as they followed others headed to the Vesta. Aster enjoyed walking through the City of Trees, winding up streets, deliberately watching out for large tree roots protruding from the ground. She almost tripped once, but Josiah's arm shot out and grabbed her before she could fall and cause any damage.

"Thanks," she mumbled, trying not to focus on the spark that went through her when he touched her.

Other groups joined theirs as they walked to the Vesta, all dressed in similar colors and fabrics, which made Aster believe this must be how they all dressed for Vesta. She noticed the older generation wore more green powder and streaks of mud across their faces than the younger couples and families. Josiah and Collin each carried a twin on their shoulders, and the laughter surrounding her from all the families with their children warmed her heart. Peace filled her entire being, and her chest eased from the stress of the past few days. Since they'd entered Cedrus, she'd felt something strange. It was like Cedrus wanted to show her something about herself. Now, as they neared the Vesta, she felt anticipation growing and swelling inside her.

Maybe Josiah is right, she thought. *Maybe I'll find what I need at the Vesta.*

They turned a corner, and Aster's breath caught.

Nestled in between the trees on the edge of town sat the Vesta.

It was like something from a dream. The building sat close to the edge of a cliff, the ravine falling off behind it to the river below. Two trees flanked a large double wooden door intricately carved with vines and flowers, which stood open, allowing the crowds to flow in and out as they pleased. The roof jutted up at a point so high that the tree branches covered the top with their leaves. As they entered, Aster noticed a large glass window serving as the back wall. The sides of the Vesta seemed to have no walls at all, but Aster realized that in between the carved wooden columns flanking the sides were raised shutters, allowing the fresh air to flow through. The openness invited the beautiful sounds of birds and the gurgling river inside, creating a natural orchestra.

Collin and Josiah let the twins down, and they quickly ran off to a group of children, all dancing and weaving among the crowd.

"Morgan, watch after them, please," Flora instructed.

Morgan nodded, taking her duties as big sister seriously. Josiah pulled her aside before she could run after them and whispered something in her ear. She went wild with excitement, and a huge smile lit up her tiny face. She nodded and ran off to join the other merry children.

"Well, Aster, what do you think?" Collin asked.

Aster searched for words from the vocabulary she'd built up over her years of extensive reading. No words could capture the beauty and awe of the Vesta. Collin took her silence as a good enough answer. He and Flora walked off and left Josiah and Aster to themselves, mingling with their friends and neighbors.

"I haven't been here for years," Josiah said, taking in the surrounding sights. "But it's just as beautiful as I remember."

The knowledge of why they were here interrupted Aster's focus on the beauty and peace surrounding her.

"Josiah," she whispered, turning to face him so others couldn't hear. "Who do you think is the spy? Should we mingle or stay in the back? Or should we…"

Josiah put his hand up to stop her rambling. "Aster, let's focus on our time here. This is important for you to experience and hear."

He motioned to where Morgan and the twins had landed with the other children.

Aster could see the children gathering around an older man, whose white hair created a stark contrast against the green forest behind him. He sat on a wooden chair by one of the open windows and beckoned the children to come near. They sat down around him, staring up at him with wide, eagerly awaiting eyes.

The adults mingled in their own groups, but Josiah led her to the man holding court with the children. Aster noticed Morgan run up to the old man. She said something to him that made him smile and nod. He patted her little hand and sent her off to sit with her brother and sister.

"Children," said the man, "today I want to tell you the story of the Knight, the King, and Ignis as it was once, long before you were born."

Aster could have sworn he glanced at her when he said this, but it happened so swiftly, she couldn't be sure. The children cheered and quieted down, ready for the story. He cleared his throat and smiled.

"Let's begin…"

He told the story superbly. The parts Aster had known and the parts she'd recently learned, all woven together, creating a wonderfully sad tale. She became so engrossed in the story, especially the part concerning Gaia and Tarron's children, and the prophecy that from their line would come the three keys to saving Ignis.

Josiah touched her arm, snapping her out of her daze, and motioned for her to follow him. As they wove their way through the crowd, she caught snippets of the adults' conversations.

"…for even now the darkness threatens to overtake us—and the Evanders are helping it along!" said one man excitedly. "First, they put our livelihoods at stake when they created the New Road, and now they want to force us to leave our homes altogether."

His listeners muttered and murmured their agreement.

"All because of what we believe!" another man cried out.

A woman in the group gave a more encouraging outlook: "We must not lose hope. They will discover the three who will free the Knight. Only he can reunite Ignis return it to its former glory!"

"That's fine, but what do we do while we wait?" a voice asked.

"We fight and defend," replied the first man.

"Perhaps," said the woman. "However, I believe we must continue searching for the three."

Aster felt awkward knowing there were some who believed

she was one of the three. She wished she could believe it and encourage these people. She felt the overwhelming amount of pressure to be the impossible.

Josiah drew her away and led her to the opposite side of the room. He pointed out the columns flanking the sides of the Vesta. Aster had noticed something carved into them, but she hadn't realized what they were until she saw them up close.

"Each column represents an important part of Ignis history," Josiah explained. "Each of these columns represents a piece of the story."

The King and Knight were carved on the first column. The carpenter had created the Knight's armor with so much detail it almost shone as the sunlight filtered down from above them.

"Let's keep walking. There's a particular one you need to see."

She tore her gaze away from the King and the Knight and followed Josiah past the other columns, picturing the story. They passed one that showed the King's Book, and Aster had an intense urge to reach out and touch it, but it felt wrong, so she kept her hands behind her back as she followed Josiah through the crowd.

He eventually stopped before reaching the glass window in the back. He grabbed Aster's hand and pulled her in for a closer look at the carvings. She saw three couples who looked like they were moving in different directions.

"These are the daughters of Gaia and Tarron and their husbands," Josiah explained. "The daughters were born with unique powers; one daughter the power of the mind, the other the power of the skies, and the third the power of the earth."

Aster's heart began beating fast as she continued to study the faces of the daughters. The anticipation building in her was reaching a breaking point.

"One daughter created an academy for Guardians in Veridi, another in Gemma, and the third daughter created one on the island of Vela," Josiah said quietly.

Aster stared intently at the face of the first daughter. The daughter's face was one she saw every time she looked in the mirror. The girl's round face, almond-shaped eyes, and curly hair resembled Aster's to a mysteriously accurate detail.

"See, Aster?" Josiah said, grabbing her hand and gazing at her. "There's no doubt you are a descendant of Gaia and Tarron, just like Mag told you. You are the Flower with a Royal Mind," he whispered breathlessly. "The King himself set your purpose. Don't you see it?"

She could hear the pleading in his voice. She couldn't believe what was staring her in the face. Realizing the King knew Gaia and Tarron's children would be the keys to destroying the darkness, and believing he'd set this path in motion, gave her a jolt of confidence. Perhaps she could do this impossible task. Seeing the faces of the other two daughters also reminded her she wouldn't be doing this alone.

"I do," she whispered back to him.

She looked at Josiah, and they both realized they were still holding hands. Instead of letting go, she gave his hand a squeeze.

He smiled back, and she could sense it relieved him. She was accepting her purpose. Though, tiny seeds of doubt still felt wedged in her mind.

"Would you like to dance?" he asked, breaking the silence between them.

"Yes, I would love that," she replied without hesitation.

They danced to the music, laughing, and enjoying the atmosphere and joy all around them. Flora and Collin found them and introduced them to their friends and neighbors. Morgan asked Josiah to dance, and he twirled her around in circles, eliciting fits of laughter from her.

The sun had set, and lanterns were lit, creating a sparkle of light throughout the dark woods. Eventually, the crowds began dispersing; the children began a chain reaction of yawns as their parents rounded them up to go home. Collin and Flora carried the twins, and Morgan walked between Josiah and Aster, holding their hands, and swinging them back and forth. They followed the trail of lanterns through streets and back to the inn.

"We'll put the children to bed, then we'll help you all get ready to leave," Collin said when they entered the inn.

"Leave?" Morgan mumbled.

"Yes, sweetie, I'm afraid we have to leave tonight," Aster

said.

"But I don't want you to leave!"

"Morgan, shh," Flora said.

Aster picked her up. "Morgan, I'm sure this won't be the last time we see you."

Morgan considered that for a moment, then nodded, too tired to argue any further. She hugged Aster and Josiah and followed her parents and siblings upstairs to bed.

"Well, we should go get changed," Josiah said as they stood in an abrupt awkward silence.

"Josiah, thank you again," Aster said.

"What you're essentially saying is that I was right?" he said with a smirk.

Aster rolled her eyes and shook her head. "Don't push it."

Chapter 12

They parted ways at their rooms. Aster changed out of the dress Flora had loaned her, laying it neatly on the bed, fingering the beautiful piece. Then she noticed an outfit folded up on the vanity, a long green blouse with a bodice to go over it, pale-green linen pants, and a long, sturdy, brown leather coat.

All Flora's doing, no doubt.

As she changed into the travel clothes, she wondered when she'd be able to return to Cedrus, if ever. She realized she'd truly miss this family who had welcomed her so warmly.

She lingered a little longer, taking in the beautiful furniture and colors. Then, she took one last look at the balcony view. Flora and Collin had lanterns lining the garden paths, and from this height, it looked like a trail of fireflies. She wished she could stay here on the balcony, in this city, forever, or at least until she found the confidence, she needed for what everyone wanted her to become.

Sighing, she went back inside, closing the balcony door behind her. She went to the kitchen and waited for the others to join her. Sitting at the table, she traced her finger over the rings that showed the age of the tree that made up this table, and she felt herself beginning to daydream, or dozing off—she wasn't sure which. Memories began resurfacing in her mind, and she was too tired to stop them. Words that had been spoken about her, and sometimes to her, played out before her eyes as if she was watching them happen to herself firsthand.

"You're so weird," a little boy from school with sun streaked, blonde hair said.

"Aster, you need to stop daydreaming and pay attention," came the voices of many adults.

"Aster stop being so strange. People never want to play with me, and it's all your fault!" her little sister cried one day on the way home from school.

Her sister's voice faded, and images began taking shape as she recalled the incident that had led to this conversation on the walk home.

Aster looked around her and realized she was dreaming of home—school, specifically.

A younger version of herself appeared, skipping into view, searching around for her sister and the other girls. Her sister and the group of girls were huddled together, hiding from her.

Aster knew what came next, and she tried to shake herself awake, but the dream pressed forward.

"Amity!" young Aster called.

"Shhh…" one of the girls instructed. "Amity, don't let her know we're over here. If she finds us, she'll want to play with us."

Amity's eyes were wide, and she didn't say a word.

"Wake up, wake up," Aster said, pinching herself, trying with all her might to avoid reliving this painful memory.

"Amity! Come on, where are you?"

Young Aster paused and looked around. She closed her eyes and concentrated.

The huddle of girls stayed out of sight, playing quietly with their dolls and making sure they stayed hidden from Aster.

Aster stared as her sister remained quiet and let the girls exclude her younger self so harshly.

"Amity," she said, knowing it was just a dream and no one could hear her, "say something."

"There you are!" young Aster said triumphantly, opening her eyes and heading for the girls' hiding spot.

The girls jumped when she approached, gave each other a look, and scattered, laughing and running away from Aster and leaving Amity behind.

"Amity?" young Aster asked, confused and hurt.

Amity's eyes brimmed with tears, and she crossed her arms. "Aster, why did you have to do that?"

"Do what?"

"You know what you did! You did that funny thing and discovered me. The girls ran off because of you."

Young Aster stood there in shock as her sister stomped off.

"Amity!" she cried, running after her. "Why did you let them treat me like that?"

Amity hmphed and walked faster, trying to lose Aster.

Aster was pulled along with the dream, with no other choice than to watch the sad story unfold.

"Amity!" young Aster cried again, hot tears now pouring down her face.

Amity swung around and glared at her.

"I don't want to play with you. I want to play with the other girls. Those girls don't become lost in their thoughts or do weird things with their mind."

Young Aster stopped in her tracks, and Amity just sighed and kept walking home, leaving Aster standing in the road, crying and heartbroken.

Aster could feel something on her face. She reached up and was startled to find tears matching those of her younger self. She felt the same emotions she'd experienced then.

Hurt.

Alone.

Misunderstood.

A freak.

She put her head in her hands to block out the scene before her. She felt the darkness around her like fingernails scratching at her skin.

"Aster, you're not who they need," a voice whispered in the darkness.

"Who's there?" she replied shakily.

"Aster, you're not strong enough for this."

"Stop," she muttered, trying to shake herself awake.

"You're just another Light Keeper who will fall to the Evanders. You're no match for the darkness."

"Sto—" she tried to say, but the words died on her lips.

"Your own family didn't believe in you. Why would anyone else?"

"STOP!" she screamed, taking her hands away from her face and yelling out in the darkness.

A voice cackled and filled her with undeniable fear. The darkness stopped scratching at her skin and began to press down on her until she could barely stand it.

She heard a voice in the distance.

"Aster, wake up."

She moaned and tried to push away the weight on her shoulders.

"Aster, wake up!" The voice grew louder as she tried pushing the weight off, and she felt a sudden sensation of falling.

Startled, she jerked awake, feeling disoriented, her face damp with sweat and her heart pounding. Josiah's face came into view. He had his hands on her shoulders, and he was staring at her intently, as though to make sure she was all right.

"Josiah?" she muttered in confusion. "What happened?"

"You were having a nightmare. I found you asleep with your head on the table. You were crying, and…" He paused.

"And what?"

"You were crying and yelling out for your sister."

Then it came flooding back to her.

"I wasn't yelling out for her," she corrected. "I was yelling *at* her."

Josiah looked at her with questions in his eyes.

Moaning, she dropped her head in her hands. "I had a dream of a memory, but it wasn't quite right."

"What do you mean?" he asked.

"I couldn't find my sister. So, I… I… used mind searching to find her, and I knew what I was doing when I did it."

"How old were you?"

"Around twelve, I think, but the thing is, I don't remember ever doing that. The way I remember it, I found her because I knew where to look."

Josiah didn't respond, just looked off, pondering her story.

"I don't know which one is real now—the dream or how I've always remembered it."

"Well," he said slowly, "you have wondered if your parents were keeping the truth from you. Maybe they did. Maybe you're beginning to remember things how they really happened."

They sat there in silence, considering the implications of what her dream might mean.

They both whipped around, startled by a sound behind them. But it was just Flora and Collin coming into the kitchen.

"What's wrong?" the ever-perceptive Flora asked.

"Nothing," Aster quickly said, before Josiah could allude to anything else.

He glanced at her, but she ignored him and got up from the table.

"Are you ready to go?" Collin asked them both.

"I am," Aster replied.

Josiah nodded. "Yes, I have the maps and a couple weapons for us both, in case of emergency." He handed Aster a small dagger for her to belt to her side.

She had never had her own dagger before, and she admired the beautiful hilt that looked like leaves intertwined together.

"Where did you get this?" she asked.

Josiah laughed. "Mag, actually. She gave me these the night before we left. She instructed me to keep them with me at all times, and that I'd know when we'd need to use them."

"Wait," said Aster, slowly realizing what he'd said, "she only gave you two. Which means she must have had a feeling we'd be separated from Roark and Andi."

"Mag is a woman of mystery," Flora interjected, "that's for sure."

Aster studied the dagger. How curious that Mag, a mind searcher herself, would have sensed the separation of their group. Aster wondered if this meant mind searchers could see into the future. She knew Mag had sent word to Flora and Collin, but to plan specifically just for her and Josiah, it made Aster wonder what else the journey had in store for them. Did Mag know they would encounter something unexpected and dangerous?

Malum's group, possibly? Aster shuddered to think.

But she couldn't let herself go there. She was still recovering from her nightmare, and she knew it wouldn't be wise to jump down another rabbit hole.

Without discussion, they gathered their things and walked quietly out the door. Flora stayed back, giving them both hugs and last words of advice.

"Be safe, trust in who you are, and have faith," she whispered into Aster's ear.

"Thank you, Flora, for everything. I'm so glad we met, and I'm sure we'll see each other again."

Flora nodded knowingly. "Yes, I think we will."

Aster gave the inn one last look and followed Josiah and Collin into the dark forest. They took the path to the Vesta, using the shadows to hide them. Collin diverted them to a small path off to the right, slopping downward toward the ravine. They each carried a lantern, but even that light barely permeated the darkness of the forest. Thankfully, beams of moonlight from above made their way down through the trees to help light their way. The brush became denser the farther they descended, and Aster almost felt claustrophobic as the tall trees with their wide trunks penned her in between them. Not to mention her feet kept slipping on the wet forest floor. The ground finally began to level out, and the brush thinned. Aster could hear the river in the distance getting closer. She peered up, standing in the bottom of the ravine. She could barely see the Vesta watching them from above. It felt like another lifetime since she and Josiah had danced in the fading light of day, and he'd showed her the carving of Gaia and Tarron's daughters.

"Here we are," Collin whispered as he led them quietly across the small dock to one of the few boats bobbing beside it.

Aster had never traveled by boat before, but it looked like a fishing boat, judging from the pictures she had seen in her books. Its green paint was peeling, but it seemed in good shape for their journey. She took their bags on board while Collin and Josiah checked to make sure the boat was ready for travel. "It's the best I could do last minute. Allow the current to tow you farther away before starting the engine," he warned.

"Thank you, Collin. I'm sorry we've put you all in possible danger, though. Please, won't you all follow us to Toparius?" Aster asked.

"Our place is here, for now. You never know, other Light Keepers might start traveling through here again. Don't worry about us, we'll be perfectly safe. And with Morgan, we won't be surprised by any unwelcome guests."

They both laughed and hugged one last time.

"Take care of him," Collin whispered for only her to hear.

She nodded and turned to leave, thankful it was dark so he couldn't see her cheeks blush. Obviously, he meant Josiah, and she wondered if Collin and Flora had noticed what she was beginning to feel between them.

Josiah and Collin said their goodbyes, and she watched them talk for a few moments but couldn't make out what they were saying. She knew it must be hard for Josiah to leave his friend, but she truly believed that if everything worked out, they'd see Collin and his family again, one day... maybe.

"Ready?" Josiah asked, coming on board.

"Ready."

Josiah took the wheel, Collin freed them from the dock, and the current began pulling them away. Aster and Josiah waved to Collin, and they watched as he became smaller and smaller until they turned a bend in the river and lost him from view.

They turned toward the front of the boat, the dark and foreboding river before them. Aster was grateful for the moonlight to help them along, especially since Josiah had her snuff out the lanterns so as not to draw attention to them.

"I thought the trees covered the river?" she asked. She wondered why so much light was making its way down on them.

"They do farther down. We'll reach that by morning, hopefully not sooner. It's dark enough under the trees. We don't need to have a dark sky added on top of it all."

They remained quiet, Josiah carefully steering the boat as it glided across the water. Now that they were safely on their way, Aster felt the adrenaline of the past few days begin to drain from her, leaving her feeling tired. But each time she almost nodded off, she became afraid of falling into the nightmare from before, and she forced herself to stay awake. She took a little of the water from her canteen and splashed it across her face, hoping to keep herself from falling asleep.

"You know if you want to sleep you can," Josiah said. He obviously thought she was trying to stay awake to help him.

"No, I'm fine, honestly. With all the excitement I couldn't imagine trying to fall asleep right now."

He shrugged his shoulders, and she was glad for the darkness so he couldn't see her face. It was always a dead giveaway when she was hiding the truth. And the truth was she felt exhausted, but she couldn't let on. Trying to keep herself awake, she decided to ask some of the thousands of questions she had swirling in her mind.

"At the Vesta," she began, "those pillars with the daughters..."

"Yes?"

"How long have you known about—what was her name?"

"Batel," Josiah replied. "Well, it's been almost eight years since I visited with Collin as his protector. I stayed with him in Cedrus before coming to Verd to join Roark and Andi. When I met you, I couldn't quite place why you looked so familiar. Then one day, the first day I caught you sneaking into school, is when I realized why I recognized you."

"I remember that day," she said quietly.

She'd awoken exceptionally late that morning after reading late the night before. She had to skip breakfast, and her stomach was growling as she ran her hidden path to the hole in the wall of the city. She'd never predicted beinggrabbed from behind after climbing through the hole.

The city wasn't quick to fix such issues, and so had put a guard on the spot instead of fixing it. Of all mornings, Josiah's duties had required him to guard the hole.

Aster had never screamed so loud before in her life. He'd surprised her so much that she thought her heart would beat out of her chest from racing so fast.

"Who are you, and what do you think you're doing?" Josiah had yelled over top of her, with his foot pinning her shoulder to the ground.

His face had registered surprise at seeing he'd apprehended a girl not much younger than himself.

"Get your foot off my shoulder!" she'd yelled back at him.

He'd hesitated but kept his stance. "Not till you tell me what you're doing sneaking into the town!"

"I'm not sneaking into town; I'm sneaking into school!" she'd moaned.

"School?"

"Yes, school, perhaps you've heard of it? It's that building right there beside us!"

"You want me to believe you're a student? You're obviously older than a student."

She'd rolled her eyes at his astute observation. "My parents started me late, because at the time, we didn't have good teachers."

She'd tried shoving his foot off but failed. "I'd love to give you the rest of my life's story, but if we're going to have a chat, I'd like to do it without your foot crushing my shoulder!"

He'd finally seemed to believe she wasn't a threat and moved his foot off.

He'd given her a hand up, but she ignored it, getting up on her own and rubbing her painful shoulder.

"Well, thank you for making me even later to school. Mr.... what's your name? I didn't quite catch it when you threw me to the ground."

"Josiah, you can call me Josiah. And I'm sorry for the confusion...?"

"Aster," a voice had said.

Roark had been standing behind them near the school with his arms crossed and that face that Aster couldn't quite read as easily as others.

"Josiah, she's no threat, just a danger to herself and her academics if she doesn't learn to be on time," Roark had said disapprovingly.

"Thanks a lot," Aster had mumbled to Josiah.

She'd picked up her bag and followed Roark back into the school to face whatever punishment he'd had in store for her this time.

"You're thinking back to when we first met, aren't you?" asked Josiah, interrupting her thoughts.

She laughed. "You know me too well.

"Which is surprising, since after our first meeting, I thought we'd never meet again, let alone become friends. I figured if you ever saw me again, you'd either try to hit me or throw something at me."

"I wouldn't have hit you after what you did the next time, I was late."

In their limited light, she could just make out Josiah's look of surprise.

"Oh, you didn't think I knew it was you?" she asked mischievously.

"I don't know what you are talking about," he said, looking off into the distance.

"So, it wasn't you who kept Roark distracted while I slipped in the back?"

He didn't say anything, but she saw the slightest smirk.

They both remained quiet after that, enjoying the companionable silence. The sounds accompanying them were a chorus of cicadas, frogs, and the water lapping against the sides of the boat.

Without meaning to, Aster's eyes became too heavy to hold up, and she fell asleep, rocked by the gentle waves and pleasant memories.

"Aster, wake up!" Josiah hissed.

She shot up and looked around as her eyes became adjusted to the light.

Light.

It's morning, she realized groggily.

She also realized she had slept, and no nightmares had attacked her. At first, she felt relief, then stiff from having lain on the hard wooden bench, and then fear when she saw Josiah's face above her. He stared off to the side, his eyes wide and mouth tight. He held the wheel tight in his grip.

Aster looked where he was staring. A man stood on the riverbank up ahead of their boat. Beyond the riverbank, she saw a tunnel of trees continuing down the river.

The Green River, she thought hopefully.

She turned her attention back to the man on the riverbank. He looked to be a traveler, probably harmless, but she understood Josiah's wariness in trusting strangers at this point. What if this person had followed them from Cedrus? Josiah had said Malum's people were known to be shape-shifters.

Could this be one of his luring them into a trap.

But surely, he wouldn't have been able to follow us on land, she thought to herself.

The man obviously had obviously seen their boat approaching. He was jumping up and down, waving his hands and yelling something they couldn't hear yet.

"What are you going to do?" Aster asked, scrambling up to stand next to Josiah as he carefully steered the boat straight ahead.

"I don't know," he answered tightly, his neck slowly disappearing into his shoulders.

She'd sensed he wanted to say something but caught himself.

"What is it?" she prodded.

"Do you think you can read his mind?"

She had a feeling he was going to ask that.

"I don't know, but I can try," she replied, secretly glad for a chance to practice in a real-life scenario.

She positioned herself so she could get a better look at the approaching figure.

She focused with all her might to read his mind, but to no avail. Maybe they were too far?

Maybe her powers weren't that strong after all?

She looked at Josiah and shook her head. "Sorry."

He nodded and kept the boat straight, making sure to keep a safe distance away from the man.

They inched closer, and Aster noticed the man's torn clothes and blood trickling down his face from a head wound. He had obviously been through trouble and probably just needed help. She could imagine how it felt to finally see help coming out of nowhere, only to have it float away, ignoring your pleas.

"Josiah, we have to help him. I think he's harmless." He glanced at her, unsure, but time was running out.

If he didn't change course now, it would be too late.

He shook his head but steered towards the man on the bank, lowering the anchor to keep the current from dragging them away. They heard the man's cries of joy the closer they got to him.

"Thank you! Oh thank you so much! You've saved me!" The man lifted his hands in joy and danced around the sandy bank.

Josiah came over, moving Aster behind him.

"Who are you? State your business here," he said with his guard voice that Aster recognized from the few times he had used it back home.

The man looked up at him from the river's edge, with wide, sorrowful eyes that penetrated Aster's heart. Something in Aster registered familiarity when she looked into his eyes. She couldn't place it, but something inside her was trying to tell her something about this stranger.

"My name is Dolion, and I was attacked by Cu-Sith just last night. I tried to fight them off, but they took everything I had. They almost took my life, but I narrowly escaped when one of their prisoners broke free while they were attacking me."

Aster gasped. Cu-Sith this far inland... with prisoners. It couldn't be a coincidence. It had to be the same ones who had attacked them.

Roark and Andi must be the prisoners!

Josiah stayed cautious despite the man's tale.

"Josiah!" Aster muttered imploringly.

He just stared a hole into the man, who was becoming more distraught realizing Josiah might deny him the help he needed.

Aster pushed Josiah aside and leaned over the edge of the boat.

"What happened to the prisoner who tried to escape? Were they a man and woman?" she asked breathlessly.

Dolion looked from Josiah to her with wide eyes.

"Yes! Yes! A man and a woman! The woman was the one who escaped. She jumped in the water and disappeared. They didn't go after her, though," he added quickly.

"Why?" Aster asked.

"Because she went into the Green River. Cu-Sith aren't mad to travel on the Green River, especially without a boat."

Aster's emotions couldn't handle much more. The Cu-Sith must believe the silly tales about the horrors and mysteries of the Green River. Their superstitions might have just saved Andi's life.

Thinking they were alive felt wonderful, but to know the Cu-Sith had taken them as prisoners was greatly disturbing. The Cu-Sith never took prisoners.

The man waded through the water, immediately stepping back, though, when Josiah's hand went to his dagger.

"When they abandoned me, I saw the briefest flash of her head bobbing up from the water. But the Green River doesn't give her a much better chance at survival. Though I suppose it's better to die by the river than by the Cu-Sith. I can show you exactly where I saw her if you let me come with you!"

Aster turned quickly to Josiah, ignoring the man's silly superstitions.

"Josiah, it has to be Andi. We have to go after her!"

Josiah looked away towards where Dolion had pointed and sighed. "Aster, we don't know if this man is telling the truth."

"I promise you my story is true!" Dolion cried.

Josiah studied him hard, but Dolion didn't waver under his scrutiny.

"Josiah!" Aster pleaded.

"Fine!" he said, throwing up his hands in defeat. "We'll take you to the end of the Green River, but that's it."

Dolion's shoulders sank. "Wait," he asked incredulously, "you're not actually going to go through the Green River, are you?"

"Yes, we are. Without or without finding our friend," Josiah retorted.

"You're crazy!" the man yelled, blood splashing off his face from his excitement.

Josiah rolled his eyes and crossed his arms, reminding Aster very much of Roark for a moment. "Do you want a ride or not? Because if you'd rather fend for yourself and live with the possibility of the Cu-Sith coming back to finish you off, then be my guest."

The man hesitated but finally nodded, though Aster couldn't read his thoughts or sense what he was truly feeling. He was obviously not sold on the idea of traveling down the mysterious Green River. This made her a little apprehensive herself, but Andi had clearly stated at Mag's that all the tales surrounding the Green River were silly superstitions.

Dolion swam to the boat, and Aster lent him a hand up. He collapsed on the hard wooden floor in relief.

"Thank you," he said, obviously glad for the assistance despite their travel route.

Aster gave him a smile and put a hand on his shoulder.

"You're welcome. Let me grab a bandage for your head wound."

Josiah raised the anchor and let the current pull them along, still not ready to try the engine so close to Cedrus. A few feet ahead of them lay the beginning of the Green River, and the trees began to form a tunnel around them the closer they got.

Josiah lit the lanterns as the trees made it harder to see, while Aster took ointment and a bandage, sitting down in front of Dolion to dress his wound.

"You're very kind, miss," he said.

She just smiled, but a question was itching its way out of her mouth.

"Why are you so afraid of the Green River? Surely, you don't believe the stories?" she asked as nicely as she could without sounding like she was mocking him.

The man stared at her as if she was crazy.

"I surely do believe them!" he declared, wincing as the ointment hit its mark. He gulped. "It's said that those who swim down the Green River go mad. The darkness makes the green blend in with the land on either side. The trees barely let in any light, and you become so disoriented that you go crazy and choose to drown rather than try to swim for one of the shores let alone try to swim the length of it. Stories say the trees come to life and drown unlucky travelers."

Aster glanced at Josiah, who had a bored look on his face. He obviously wasn't concerned about the superstitions, so she decided she would try not, be either. Though the way Dolion talked as they entered the ominous, dark, green tunnel, it was hard not to believe them. She finished bandaging Dolion and left him to go have a word with Josiah.

"Don't start believing in superstitions, Aster," he said before she could get a word out.

She crossed her arms, angry at him for assuming, and angry that he was right again.

"Fine," she muttered to herself. "But all superstitions have a measure of truth to them."

They would soon find out, because they entered the Green River just moments later. The light dimmed, and what light they did have from above glowed green.

Aster peered down, seeing the green waters for the first time. They did glitter like emeralds in the rays of light that snuck between the tree branches above.

"It's beautiful," she said quietly to herself.

"Beautiful and treacherous," Dolion said from behind her.

She hadn't heard him and tried to hide the fact that he'd startled her. She didn't wish to be rude, but she needed to be wise. It felt foolish to blindly trust a stranger they'd picked up on the side of the river.

"I just want us to find Andi. If anyone can make it, it's her," Aster said. "Where do you think they were taking the other prisoner, our other friend?"

"I'm not sure." Dolion shrugged. "I've never known the Cu-Sith to come this far inland, and I've never heard of them taking prisoners. Who knows where they're headed, but your friends must be important if they kept them alive?"

Aster felt Dolion's piercing eyes examining her intently. She shifted uncomfortably under his scrutiny but didn't reply to his assumption.

"What did you say your names are?"

"We didn't," Josiah said from the wheel. He didn't even look at Dolion, but his comment made clear to Aster that he didn't want her to give Dolion any information about them. It was hard for her to see people as threats. She supposed as a guard and living on the run, it must be habit for Josiah.

Dolion nodded, accepting Josiah's unspoken terms. "Well, I thank you both for allowing me to ride with you, even if it's only till the end of the Green River."

Aster studied him closely. She couldn't read his thoughts to know if he was attempting to garner sympathy or if he spoke honestly.

"Where were you headed before the Cu-Sith attacked you?" she asked.

"I was headed to Toparius. I'm hoping to get a job on a fishing boat. My family disappeared when we became separated by a recent storm."

"I'm so sorry," Aster replied.

"Thank you," Dolion said quietly. "I want to find peace, and I believe I can find it working on the sea."

"I've heard it's beautiful."

"You've never seen it?"

"No, but I've read about it, and I've seen pictures. I heard you can see the edge of the Vela shores."

"It's true," Dolion said excitedly. "I saw that for myself once when I was quite young. My father worked as a fisherman and took me out with him one day. The sun was bright, and the sea matched the blue of the sky. Suddenly, I saw a shape forming on the horizon, and there it was—Vela. Even at a distance, seeing a new land felt freeing."

Aster noticed Dolion sounded far off in his memories, and she thought she sensed a hint of regret and longing as well. But she still couldn't sense his thoughts, let alone read them to know for sure what he was thinking or feeling.

"Yes, I'm sure it did." Aster sighed.

She was beginning to trust Dolion more, and she wondered what other stories he could tell them.

Though she couldn't read Dolion, she could clearly read and sense Josiah's thoughts on their new addition. He did not like or trust Dolion.

He called for Aster to come join him at the wheel. "You need to stop wasting time chatting with that stranger and keep your eyes peeled for Andi. Remember her? She's the reason we even let this man on the boat."

Aster rolled her eyes. "Of course, I remember her, and I'm sorry I was having a conversation instead of ignoring the man. You've been near the shores-maybe try to connect with him instead of treating him like a rat on ship."

She almost walked off, but her anger got the better of her.

"If you assume I don't care about finding Andi, then you don't know me after all."

She left him with his mouth open and eyebrows in a scowl. She didn't care to hear what he had to tell her. She understood his apprehension of Dolion, but how dare he question her caring for Andi's safety. It broke her heart to think Andi was out here alone, possibly struggling to stay alive.

Dolion said one would rather die alone in the Green River than killed by the Cu-Sith.

Thinking of the Cu-Sith, though, made her mind start whirling with thoughts on why they had kept Roark and Andi as prisoners. The Cu-Sith were mercenaries when they weren't thieving just for fun. Did someone hire them to find her? Who, though? The bigger question remained, were these really Cu-Sith or something deadlier?

Help!

Aster gasped as the cry for help interrupted her thoughts.

She whirled around, her eyes wide and searching. Dolion was staring at the water. Josiah kept one eye on Dolion and the other on the river. They weren't the source of the cry.

She closed her eyes and focused on the sound of the person's thoughts. She didn't want to cry wolf before making sure.

Help! the voice cried out again.

Who's there? Where are you? But Aster remembered the person could only answer if they were a mind searcher.

Which they obviously weren't, since she heard no reply.

Aster attempted to decipher where the cry came from.

She ran back to Josiah, who immediately noticed her panicked face.

"What's wrong?" he whispered, not wanting to attract Dolion's attention.

"I hear someone crying out for help," she whispered so Dolion wouldn't hear.

"Andi?" Josiah asked hopefully.

Aster shrugged. "I can't be sure."

"Where is it coming from?"

"I don't know, but it's getting louder from when I first heard it a minute ago."

"Okay, that means we have to be getting closer, right?"

"I think so."

She closed her eyes again and concentrated on the sound of the voice, the grass and trees surrounding them, the sound of the water beneath them. Then, as if someone had placed a picture in front of her face, she saw a figure holding on to the roots of a tree, their legs dangling in the river. She couldn't quite make out the person's face, but behind them she saw a shape looming closer, and she gasped upon realizing it was their boat she saw coming up behind the person.

"Up ahead!"

Josiah steered them off their straight path, and Aster grabbed the lantern, hurrying over to the side. The cry for help grew louder every second, and not just in her head. She noticed Josiah and Dolion heard it now as well.

They edged closer to the figure, and Aster could see it was a woman.

"Andi!" Aster shouted.

The woman's head turned, and Aster cried out in satisfaction. It was Andi! Her face lit up with a smile of relief and joy.

"Aster! Josiah!" she called back.

Dolion rushed over to join Aster. "I can't believe it! You were right about your friend—she's quite strong to survive this long out here."

"Josiah, you have to get closer!" Aster called back to him, ignoring Dolion's comment.

"If I move closer, the riverbank will clip the side of the boat."

He struggled with the wheel, trying to gauge how close he could get for Aster and Dolion to help Andi onto the boat.

Aster ran and grabbed the rope from the other side. A sudden thought assaulted her. They were almost right next to Andi, and she knew they only had one chance at rescuing their friend.

"Andi, let go with one hand and catch this rope!" Aster threw the rope, and Andi reached out but missed by a few inches.

Aster threw it again, and this time Andi caught it, letting go of the branch simultaneously, causing her to splash down into the green water.

"ANDI!" Aster yelled out in dismay.

She threw off her jacket to jump in.

"Aster, don't you dare!" Josiah yelled.

She ignored him and had her hand on the edge of the boat, but Dolion grabbed her around the waist and pulled her back.

"No! Josiah's right, you can't go in that water!" he warned ominously.

She struggled against him, but he held tight to her. He put one hand around her waist, and the other he used to grab the rope and pull it back. The slack rope pulled taught, and Andi's head surfaced from under the water.

Aster relaxed in Dolion's grip, relieved to see her friend alive. Dolion let go of Aster, and together they pulled Andi up into the boat.

Andi lay on the floor, coughing and sputtering, trying to catch her breath. Aster sat down, exhausted but at the same time feeling adrenaline continue to course through her veins.

She couldn't believe they'd found Andi.

"Good. Job." Andi got out between gasps, smiling up at her.

She grabbed Aster's hand and gave it a squeeze, sighing and closing her eyes. Aster could tell her journey since being with the Cu-Sith, plus escaping, had worn her out.

But Andi didn't stay down long. She pushed herself up off the floor of the boat, her long, black, braided hair dripping wet. Dolion held out a hand to help her. She looked at him curiously but didn't ask any questions.

Aster didn't think, just grabbed her up in a tight hug.

"I thought you were dead!" Aster whispered, surprised to feel tears pooling in her eyes.

"Oh, Aster, you should know me better than that. I'm not going down that easily."

Aster laughed, then Andi, and neither could stop.

Finally, Aster took a breath to calm herself and felt her friend's scrutiny.

"You're different," Andi remarked, looking at her curiously.

Aster shifted on her feet and glanced quickly at Dolion. Andi seemed to understand and just nodded. They could talk about their separate journeys soon, but not with a stranger on board and within earshot.

"Andi, this is Dolion," Aster said, introducing the two. They shook hands.

"You're the one the Cu-Sith attacked while we were with them, aren't you?" Andi asked.

"Yes, and thanks to your escape, they left me instead of killing me. I think they were more concerned with getting your friend off before he escaped as well. If they hadn't, I wouldn't have been able to tell your friends you were alive somewhere on the river."

"Well, thank you. Thank you, all," Andi said, wrapping her arm around Aster. Aster knew Andi had to be wondering about Roark's fate.

Andi began looking around and saw Josiah at the wheel. "Josiah!"

She and Aster walked over to him; the three friends reunited.

"I'm so sorry, Andi, it's all my fault," Josiah said. Aster's heart wrenched at the sound of a catch in his voice.

Andi held him at arm's length and gave him a long, hard look.

"Josiah, don't you dare do that. Don't you dare take blame for something out of your control. Plus, your job was to keep her safe, not us. You followed the instructions we gave you."

He nodded and looked down, trying to hide his face which threatened to reveal his emotions.

Aster smiled, glad that they'd found Andi, glad that Josiah's guilt could be alleviated some.

"What happened after we left?" Josiah asked Andi.

She sighed. "Well, it was strange. Many of the Cu-Sith were out cold after Aster…" Andi glanced at her briefly. "After Aster distracted them. Roark broke free and fought with their leader, but the other Cu-Sith came and helped overpower him, and they pinned us down. We were just outnumbered. I figured that would be the end of it, but instead they tied us up, blind folded us and dragged us, behind them. We walked for two days. I started hearing the faint sound of the water, and I figured we were close to the Green River, maybe even Cedrus. I think somehow they knew you would take this route."

Josiah hung his head, and Aster figured he was remembering back to his argument with Roark concerning their route and not trusting Roark's plan.

Andi put a hand on Josiah's shoulder, noticing his conflict. "You were right to travel through Cedrus, Josiah. It looks like you found the help there that you needed."

"We did," Aster answered for him. "We met Collin and Flora, actually."

Andi smiled. "Oh good! That means you were in good hands. I trust them with my life."

She looked at Aster with a question in her eyes, but Aster could tell she decided it was best to wait and ask later.

"Like I said," Andi continued, "I began hearing the river, the first sound I had heard for those two days, because the Cu-Sith aren't exactly chatty. I have no clue what their intentions were—or are. The next thing I knew, they began whispering about hearing travelers ahead of us. I was so worried it would be you all. I realize now it was Dolion. They went after him, and Roark somehow cut the ropes on my wrists and pushed me away. He whispered, "Run!" and that's what I did. I jumped in the water and swam for the entrance of the Green River. I just hoped they would believe the old superstitions and not follow after me."

"Good thing for you they did," Josiah said. "So, you don't know where they were taking you or why they kept you prisoners?"

Andi shook her head. "No, I wish I did. They didn't talk the entire journey. At night, when they made camp, they placed us in a tent away from theirs."

Josiah looked crestfallen. Aster felt the same. If they learned where the Cu-Sith were headed, they might have a chance at saving Roark.

"It doesn't sound like they were traveling to Cedrus, so Flora and Collin should be safe," Aster said, trying to sound positive.

"My guess is they're headed for Venari, but that seems out of their way, to be so close to the Green River," Andi said, frustrated.

"The expansion after the recent storms stretched Venari's territory," Dolion interrupted. "I apologize, I didn't mean to overstep, but I heard you talk about the Cu-Sith, and I believe they could still be headed to Venari."

"What makes you think that?" Josiah asked with obvious distrust.

"Well, Andi didn't hear them talk, but I did. I was camped nearby the night before they found me. I heard voices and went to investigate. When I saw it was the Cu-Sith, I immediately hid. But I stayed close to hear what they had to say."

"And?" Josiah asked.

"They said something about needing Andi and the other one. Roark, was his name, you said? Needing them for someone. He paid them to grab four people."

"He?"

"Yes, he. They never mentioned a name, but they referred to the person in charge as a he."

"Did they say anything else?"

"Well, let me think. I know I heard the word Light Keeper, and…" Dolion stopped, his face contorted in an effort of remembering.

"And?" Josiah pushed him harshly.

"Josiah," Andi chided.

"I'm sorry, that's all I can remember," Dolion said apologetically. Dolion looked between the trio, obviously hoping for answers, and maybe catching the sense that they were not telling him something.

Josiah turned his attention to Aster. "You and Andi get some rest in the cabin below. I'll keep watch."

"I can help," Dolion offered, but Josiah ignored him and kept his eyes peeled ahead.

Aster was about to reprimand his lack of manners, but he seemed to sense it before she said it.

"Dolion," Josiah said with a roll of his eyes, "thank you, helping us find Andi. And for keeping Aster from foolishly jumping intothe water."

Dolion nodded appreciatively, and Aster felt the ice melt between them, at least one layer.

She rolled her eyes at Josiah but couldn't keep a grin off her face, following Andi to the small cabin below them. They also found an extra lantern, giving them better light than from the small windows on either side.

"I'm so glad we found you, Andi," Aster said, curling up on one of the two cots.

Andi sat across from her, sighing as she leaned her head back against the wall of the boat. "I knew you would."

"How?" Aster asked, lighting the lantern, setting it carefully on the table.

"I had faith."

"Faith." Aster repeated the word that she had heard often from Josiah over the past few days.

"Yes," Andi said, bemused. "Still struggling to believe you're made for this?"

"I'm beginning to believe," Aster admitted.

Aster told Andi about what she had discovered at the Vesta, and her encounter with Morgan. When she finished, she sighed, exhausted from reliving it all.

"What is it?" Andi asked.

"This all seems so impossible," Aster answered. "I believe the Knight is real. I believe there's a solution to save Ignis, but the impossible part of it all is that somehow I am a part of that solution. All my life I've felt purposeless. Now, I have a purpose, with lives depending on me fulfilling that purpose."

She caught her breath, realizing how much she'd needed to get that out of her system.

"How do I do this, Andi? How do I become what everyone needs me to be? Andi?"

She looked and smiled, realizing Andi had fallen asleep. That was fine. Her speech didn't feel completely useless. She felt better getting those feelings off her chest. At home, she would have journaled her feelings, but it felt good saying them out loud and not hearing more opinions from others.

Besides, she knew what Andi's answer would be.

"Have faith."

Chapter 13

Aster woke to see light streaming down in green lines. Andi's cot was empty, and she could hear voices whispering above her.

Aster went outside and was surprised to see the tress had thinned above their heads, the overarching branches feeling less like a dark cave and more like an inviting tunnel with an intricately woven ceiling. Sunliight poured in from above and cascaded in waterfalls of light like emerald and jade, bouncing off the water.

"Beautiful, isn't it?" Andi asked from behind her.

"My books never actually could do the real world justice. Don't get me wrong," Aster added, "I wouldn't trade my books for anything, but since I left home, I'm realizing I need a bit of both."

"You're growing up with every mile," Andi said proudly. "By the way, Josiah told me about your nightmare before you left Flora and Collin's."

Aster sighed. "I should have told you last night, but I didn't feel like I could handle it yet."

Andi pulled her away to the front of the boat, trying to avoid Dolion's sharp ears.

"Aster, tell me," Andi said.

Aster described the dream, the hurt just as strong as when she first experienced it.

"Andi, I promise I don't remember using my ability that young. The rest of the dream was accurate." She paused. "I explained to Mag I've felt like there's a veil on my memories. I only see half of what happened. Until the other night. Last night, I believe I saw my first complete memory."

Andi sat anxiously, wringing out her wet braids and looking out on the Green River.

"What did Mag say?" Andi asked.

"Mag told me not to push myself. She said I might not like what I recover. She told me I need to be sure I can handle it."

Andi nodded. "I'd heed her advice, then. Don't push yourself to see the full picture, at least not yet. I'm genuinely more worried about the suddenness of the nightmare. Is that the only one you've had since then?"

"Yes. I was tired and overwhelmed. I think the stress got to me."

"Hmmm," Andi replied warily. "Be careful, and pay attention to the nightmares. For you, nightmares aren't always just nightmares."

Aster felt confused. "What do you mean? What else could they be?"

Andi didn't answer, just looked off in the distance.

"Andi?"

"Hmm?"

"What do you mean that for me, nightmares aren't just nightmares?"

"It's a lot to explain, especially here, where the boat has ears," Andi said, nodding back toward Dolion, who was trying to engage Josiah in conversation. This reminds me. Have you taken time to read through the journal?"

Aster shifted uneasily.

"I have read some—and I remembered it when I tried to helping find Morgan. I find it fascinating that mind searchers can telepathically communicate with each other."

"Well," Andi said, "you need to read the journal as thoroughly as you read your books at home."

Andi reached into the rucksack and handed the leather journal to Aster. She stared at the heavy book she'd found by accident. Her discovery felt like a lifetime ago.

"Before you open it," Andi said, with a sudden thought, "I want you to just hold it and concentrate on the journal itself. Similar to your interaction with Morgan and the Knight's last letter."

Aster nodded. "I'll try."

Andi smiled. "I'm going to keep our guest occupied, just in case he decides to start questions. Go to the cabin where you'll have privacy. I want to know more about our new friend."

They both glanced at Dolion, trying, and failing to engage Josiah in conversation, and laughed at the annoyed look on Josiah's face.

Following Andi's advice, she sat down in the cabin, holding the journal with closed eyes. She almost gave up, feeling like the exercise was fruitless, when a calm filled her as she focused her thoughts on where she had found the journal.

Her family's library.

One of her favorite places to find comfort and solace.

The surrounding noises dimmed to a whisper so soft that she couldn't hear anything. Her fingertips felt warm, but it was a comfortable warmth, unlike the untamable fire. A light began growing in front of her, despite her closed eyes. It grew and grew, so bright she had to turn her head.

It disappeared in a flash.

She turned her head back and gradually peeked open her eyes.

She saw a room lined with shelves, a fire crackling in the fireplace. The room looked familiar, but she couldn't quite place it; then it hit her. She was standing in her family's library, but not what she was used to it looking like. Aster could only think it must be when her great-grandmother, the journal's previous owner, had lived in the house.

She almost jumped when she realized someone else was in the room with her. A man sat at her family's desk, scribbling something in the journal. The same journal she held in her hands back on the boat.

Aster knew it was just a dream, a memory from the journal itself. She walked around the room, exploring the differences time had created.

Aster glanced out the window and felt shocked to see how different it looked. The sky was brighter, the forest less thick, and there was just a sapling where their tree house would one day stand. She turned her attention to the man at the desk. By the looks of it, he was her great-grandfather. A woman darted into the room.

Her great-grandmother.

"Have you finished copying with it?" she asked him desperately.

"Almost," he replied without glancing up.

"We have to hurry. If we don't leave soon, it will be too late."

The man scribbled one last thing, slammed the journal shut, and handed it to the woman, who jammed it into her satchel.

"Now let's be off before.-"

But the woman didn't finish her sentence as a banging downstairs startled them both.

Aster whirled around and peeked out the window. Her stomach dropped when she saw who it was attempting to barge inside.

Cu-Sith!

"Run!" she yelled at her great-grandparents, but of course they couldn't hear her.

They looked helplessly at each other. The man nodded soberly.

"I won't leave you," the woman said, shaking her head emphatically.

"Go!" he said, grabbing another journal off the desk and handing it to her.

Aster saw tears in his tired eyes.

He pushed her toward the shelf beside the fireplace and pulled a book off the middle shelf, and the secret door Aster had discovered for herself just days ago opened, revealing the hidden staircase.

"Go! You must get the journals to the Academy. You know the plan. If the information fails to reach the Academy, they won't find the Knight, and Ignis will remain separated."

They had no time for last farewells. He pushed her into the hidden room, slammed the door on her, and waited to meet his fate.

Aster abruptly found herself on the staircase with the woman.

Sobbing softly, the woman laid her hand on the hidden door. Voices roared below and made their way up to the library, doors slamming and glass shattering.

"Where is it?" a muffled voice yelled.

"Darkness will never overcome. The light will always win," her great-grandfather responded resolutely.

One of the Cu-Sith slapped him so hard she heard him fall to the ground.

"No matter how long you try to keep a candle burning, it will melt away, forgotten, useless. Then it will melt away into nothingness. Today you have died in vain."

A loud snap filled the air, then silence.

Aster gasped and staggered back, falling down the steps into the inky blackness below. It felt like she fell for hours, but she landed on the ground, tumbling out into a meadow, unscathed. She looked up and saw her great-grandmother walking into a clearing.

Mag's clearing, Aster realized.

Mag ran out to meet her. She fell into Mag's arms and passed out with grief. Mag looked up.

Aster caught her breath. She felt Mag staring at her as if she knew she was there. The world began spinning around her, making her dizzy.

The meadow disappeared, and in its place, a gigantic wall of greenery appeared in front of her. She looked around for her great-grandmother. There she stood; her face hopeful yet full of sorrow. She took a deep breath, stepped forward, and pushed against the green wall; it moved at her touch, a small opening revealing itself like a door. She stepped in, and Aster followed her.

They walked down a narrow path paved with beautiful stones that sparkled with morning dew. They rounded corners and trudged up little stone steps before the path faded off and opened to the bottom of a hill. Once they crested the hill, the woman stopped and took a breath.

Before them lay a beautiful vista of rolling green hills, the sea sparkling in the distance, and a castle nestled in the middle.

Aster realized this was the Academy, during her great-grandmother's lifetime.

It was a beautiful sight to behold.

The woman's shoulders relaxed as if someone had lifted a weight off them, and Aster could feel her emotions shift from nervous to peaceful.

The memories began changing again, each quicker than the next.

Two small children raced outside to meet the woman.

"Momma!" they yelled.

The woman sobbed and held them tight.

Then they were inside the Academy, this time following the two children as they aged and worked through their classes, their practices with their ability, and meditation.

Her great-grandmother handed the journal to the girl. The young girl looked at it with wide eyes and nodded.

The young girl aged, and Aster watched as she handed it to another young girl, whom Aster recognized instantly as her own mother.

Her mother stood taller as she held the journal and said, "I promise to keep searching for the Light."

Then Aster's father appeared, younger, and with a face full of hope for the future.

But something shifted, the scenes growing darker.

Aster felt a disturbance in the memory's air. Her mother's and father's faces told her something felt wrong with them as well.

"We have to escape, now."

"But we can't leave! Our family lives here, our children are safe here. They'll learn about the light in safety."

"Is it safe for them here, though?" her father asked.

"What are you suggesting?"

"That we've done our part, we've tried to keep the Light, we've told the children the story. Let's leave here before the Evanders make it impossible. Or worse, the storms reach us in this place."

"But that means abandoning everything we've ever believed," her mother said in dismay.

"No, no," he bargained. "It just means we move to Verd, your family's home.. Where they won't suspect us of being different, of being a part of something they deem dangerous."

Her mother looked at him in horror, and Aster's heart twisted at the thought of her father forcing her mother to make such a decision.

Her father grabbed her mother's hands and said quietly, "One day the Knight will return, and we'll be ready, safe and sound with our family intact, and we'll enjoy a united Ignis. Together. But if we stay here…"

His voice trailed off, leaving no question of what he was implying.

Aster watched her mother struggle with her warring thoughts, but eventually she sighed and nodded. Aster groaned. She watched as her parents packed their things and took their family away from the Academy in the dark of night.

Aster fell to her knees and put her head in her hands. Not only did they know about her ability, but they were also once Light Keepers themselves. When she opened her eyes again, she found herself back in the library.

"See, we made the right decision," her father said.

"I suppose," her mother responded, rocking a baby, whom Aster realized was her little sister, Amity.

"We need to be careful, though, and watch Aster. I think she might be coming into her ability."

"But isn't that a good thing?"

"No!" he said harshly. He sighed and added softly, "I mean, not this far from the Academy. I thought leaving the Academy would prevent her powers from developing further. And we're not the ones to teach her about it."

"We can use the journal," her mother said.

"Maybe, but not till she's ready. We'll watch and decide when the environment is safe for Light Keepers."

"We can't lie to her. If she does have powers, she'll be asking questions."

"I know, but for her own good, for her safety and ours, we'll tell her it's just daydreaming or something. If she focuses more on reality and less on her dreams, then maybe it will help dampen her powers."

Her mother gasped.

"At least until it's safe," her father quickly added.

"NO!" Aster cried out.

She forced herself out of the memory. She fell to the floor of the boat and tossed the journal from her hands like it was on fire.

Josiah burst through the door; he glanced at the journal laying on the floor away from Aster. He paused at the doorway, then stuck his head back outside.

"She's fine, she just saw a spider," he fibbed, ducking his head as he entered the cabin, shutting the door behind him.

"What's wrong? What did you see?" he asked quietly, sitting next to her.

Aster realized she was drenched in sweat and her breathing was labored. She shook her head. All she could picture were the haunting memories the journal had showed her.

Her lungs felt incapable of holding any air. She shot up off the bed and paced around the cabin, gasping for air, feeling a vise tighten around her chest. She couldn't sit, she couldn't stand; she couldn't think clearly.

"I can't breathe," she finally managed to say.

"Aster, you are panicking," Josiah said, standing up and holding her still with his firm hands on her arms. "Take a deep breath."

She shook her head; didn't he realize she couldn't?

"Yes, you can!" he said firmly. He took a deep breath. "In. Out. In. Out."

She followed his prompting, and finally, after a minute or two, she felt the vise loosen and her brain fill with oxygen again.

"There," he said. He Led her back to the cot. "Take another deep breath and tell me what you saw."

"My father took us from the Academy," she finally managed to say. "He let fear cloud his judgement. He preferred to be 'normal.' I suppose he wanted his family to be normal as well."

She looked up at Josiah, stricken, as it fully hit her.

"He's the one who decided to not tell me about my ability. He told my mother he just wanted to dampen it until it was safer, but that's not what he intended at all. He never wanted me to become a Nimus. He didn't want me asking questions," she added bitterly.

As her anger rose inside her, she pulled her hands through her hair in frustration. "I hate that I picked up that stupid journal when I found it. I hate that I told you about it. I hate that I met Mag. I hate all of this!"

The sobs racked her body, and she couldn't get another word out.

Josiah put his arm around her and pulled her close. Aster attempted to push him away. She didn't want him to comfort her; she wanted to stay angry. But he held her tightly in his arms and whispered soothingly for her to calm down and take a deep breath.

"Listen," he said quietly, "I know this hasn't been easy. It's new, strange, and becoming scary. I get that. But remember the Vesta and what you learned. You were made for this. This is your purpose."

"Maybe my father knew I couldn't handle it, and that's why he forced us to be normal. Maybe there's some other memory I'm repressing."

This time Josiah held her away from him, made her look into his eyes. "Look, no disrespect, but your father was wrong. He was wrong to leave the Academy, and he was incredibly wrong to try to dampen your powers. But are you going to let his mistake, his fear, control you now? Do you want to repeat his mistake? Or will you wipe the tears away and start studying the journal and become who you're supposed to be?"

Aster just stared back at him, shocked at his brash honesty, in awe of his empowering speech. He looked back at her and shrugged.

"Well? The choice is yours. But you have to decide," he said, letting go of her.

She didn't fall when he let go. Instead, she steadied herself, wiped away the remaining tears, and reached down for the journal off the floor.

"If you don't mind, I'd like to be alone, please."

He looked at her with a raised eyebrow. "What are you going to do?"

She stared at him, mustering the best smile she could. "I will not make the same mistake my father did. I'm going to run toward the Light, not away from it. And, of course, I'm going to read," she added with a smirk.

Josiah smiled and went to leave. Aster grabbed his hand before he made it to the door.

She gazed up at him.

"Josiah… I…." She couldn't seem to form the words to thank him.

He seemed to understand. "You're welcome."

Chapter 14

The Green River took them through Veridi at a good clip. They could bypass not just Venari but any unwelcome surprises from Cu-Sith or outlying villages between Cedrus and Venari that might not welcome strangers. People had become quite territorial with each new storm devouring the land. Aster used this time to pore over her great-grandmother's journal. She felt empowered by the knowledge she gained with each passing day. Gradually, her confidence grew, and she didn't feel as overwhelmed by the weight of responsibility. As she read, she discovered the responsibility was less on her and the other two keys. It all depended on the Knight himself. They were just the ones who would help find him. Only he could restore Ignis. She and the others were just stepping stones toward that goal.

Realizing it wasn't just on her shoulders or the others, she felt a sense of relief and weightlessness that she hadn't felt since Andi and Roark had told her everything in his office back at the school.

When she wasn't reading the journal, she and Andi discussed more about Light Keepers, far away from Dolion, who remained an unknown entity to them.

"So, according to the journal," Aster discussed with her one day, "my power comes from a willingness to believe?"

"You've almost got it," Andi confirmed. "We are all born with what my mother called a spark. We can fan the spark into a flame, coax it into a small light, or let it become a forest fire. Or let it go out altogether. Fear kept some from it, like you, and forced Light Keepers to hide their powers. Others don't know or care about their spark. They let it blow away. They lose out on so much when they don't choose to embrace the gift they've been born with. The thing with a spark is that it can sometimes start a forest fire. The forest fire is you, and the other two Light Keepers."

"Isn't a forest fire a bad thing?" Aster asked.

"Yes, if left unchecked, it can consume everyone and everything around it. Those are the Cu-Sith."

"Wait," Aster interrupted, "the Cu-Sith were Light Keepers?"

Andi sighed. "Some were, yes. Others grew up with Light Keeper parents, and they came to hate everything to do with it. The thing I want you to remember, Aster, is this: forest fires can also help vegetation grow, create a rebirth."

Aster didn't see herself as a forest fire. But she hoped the more she read and practiced, she'd find the fire inside her.

Though she found practicing hard to do with Dolion on board. She and Andi would go below deck together at night saying they were going to bed, even though it was still quite early, and Andi allowed Aster to practice her mind searching on her. She started out reading Andi's thoughts, then she advanced to walking through them, exploring her mind to an extent. Andi even agreed she'd let Aster try to dive into her dreams one night—another aspect of her powers she discovered from reading her great-grandmother's journal. She also studied the drawings. Some were of the people her great-grandmother met, some were maps of Ignis before the earthquake. The drawing that caught Aster's interest the most was a painting of a beautiful vista of rolling hills, flowers, a clear stream, and blue skies. It was the same vista she had been seeing in her dreams, with one difference. Her great-grandmother's painting had a large mansion on the top of the farthest hill. Aster admired the artist's detailed handiwork. She could have sworn she saw a tiny person standing in the window of a tower. She asked Andi if she recognized the scene.

"Of course!" she said. "That's the Academy of Veridi, in Toparius. Oh how I miss it." She fondly traced the picture.

"I am excited to see it in person-again," Aster said, remembering the truth of her past and the few years she'd spent in the Academy herself before her father took them away. She gazed at the picture that had captured her dreams for so long now.

"I just hope it's still in one piece when we get there," Andi whispered.

"Wait—what do you mean?" Aster asked, concerned.

Andi sighed. "I'm not sure, but Roark said he heard rumors the Academy was in danger of being discovered. Plus, there's always the possibility of a storm hitting it, but they've never hit in that area."

"We'll just have to have faith that everything is okay," Aster said.

Aster also practiced on Josiah, without him knowing. She tried not looking at him. She discovered it was harder to search someone's mind if they weren't a mind searcher. What she discovered with Josiah surprised her. He wasn't as sure of himself as he let on, and he worried about Roark's fate. Aster knew he said he'd been close to Andi and Roark, but she hadn't realized how much of a brother and father figure Roark had been for him since they met at the Academy. She understood his concern, but she tried to get his mind distracted by talking when she wasn't practicing on him. She also asked him to teach her about the boat. She had read books about them, but she learned better seeing things firsthand. They laughed, and it reminded her of how their friendship was before things became so complicated.

"I know what you're doing," Josiah said one day as she tried to practice reading his thoughts without looking at him.

"What do you mean?" She asked.

"You make a face every time you try to read someone's mind. I noticed it just now before you looked away."

She stuck out her tongue at him. "I do not make a face."

I don't, do I? she wondered. It wouldn't do to have people know what she was doing, thinking she was sick, or worse, thinking she was crazy.

"Yes, you do. I'm sure you'll learn to control it with time and practice."

"I have been practicing! I should have it down better," she groaned, throwing her head down on her lap.

"You've only been practicing a few days, and even at that, Andi says you're doing well. I mean, you've evidently made progress, since fire doesn't come out of your hands anymore."

She grimaced, remembering the slight hole right below Josiah's feet in the cabin where she had practiced. The sparks had continued to emit from her fingers when she delved deep into her thoughts. Once her hand shot up, accidentally putting a hole in the boat's floor above. Thankfully, Josiah stepped aside to look at the river. Or he would have a sorch mark on him, or worse.

One of the first things a Light Keeper learning their ability had to do was learn to control it. And she had read most beginners experienced the sparks coming out of their hands and the taste of iron in their mouths. Andi said it wasn't a typical power Nimus's showed, but she'd expected Aster's powers to be different than the typical.

"Just another sign that you're special," Andi had said.

Aster took the encouragement but was also careful to not become cocky. She hoped the rest would come as easily.

One evening after supper- fish, again, Josiah waited for Dolion to move to the end of the boat where he slept, then motioned for Andi and Aster to come closer.

"We're getting closer to the end," he said.

"Shouldn't we be happy about that?" Aster asked, confused by his somber attitude.

He shook his head and Andi spoke of his fear.

"Once we get out of the Green River, we'll be an easy target for the Cu-Sith, if they're nearby."

"Plus, there's the problem with our baggage," Josiah said.

"You mean Dolion?" Aster asked.

"Of course, I mean Dolion," Josiah replied, becoming more frustrated. "I told him we would take him to the end of the Green River. I made the bargain for Andi's sake. We're about to discover whether he'll leave or if I'll have to throw him off."

"Josiah!" the two women reprimanded him.

"Hey!" he said. "I don't trust him. There's something about him that's given me a bad feeling from the beginning. It hasn't gone away once."

"He is rather quiet and mysterious," Andi conceded.

"But that doesn't mean he has nefarious plans," Aster defended. "We haven't been the most welcoming hosts," she said, glaring at Josiah.

He put his hands up in defense. "I'm just trying to be cautious."

"You're trying to be Roark." Aster let the words leave her mouth before she realized what she was saying. "Josiah, I'm so sorry, I didn't mean..."

It was too late. The hurt in his eyes said it all.

He spun around and walked away from them.

Andi gave her a look. *Why did you have to go there?*

Aster sighed and walked over to Josiah.

He didn't acknowledge her.

"Josiah, I'm sorry," she said. "I know you're struggling with not knowing where he is, and I know you feel bad for how you left things."

"Oh, and you know that because you dug around in my mind?" he shot back.

Aster took a step back. His eyes and tone scared her. It wasn't the Josiah she knew.

"You know what," he continued, "I'm sick of you digging around my mind and reading my thoughts without asking. You practice your stuff on Andi, and that's one thing, but you doing it to me without asking is another. It's rude, and it's invasive. And it's just plain weird," he added, sounding childish.

She could have handled all his ranting, but the last word he chose cut her deep, and he knew it the moment he said it. He knew how her friends and family had made her feel. She turned to leave; she didn't want him to see her cry.

But her stubbornness didn't want him to have the last word.

She straightened her shoulders and looked him square in the face. "No, Josiah, I didn't know all of that because I dug inside your mind. Did doing so confirm what I already knew? Yes. But I knew that stuff because I know you. We've always been able to read each other. You're my... I thought you were my friend. But I see now I was wrong."

She didn't let him reply. She turned around and stalked off to the cabin, letting tears stream down her face. Once she entered the cabin, she crumpled into a ball. The one person who had always accepted her oddity, now calling her weird. Even in the heat of anger, he knew his arrow would press her to the core.

A knock sounded on the door. Aster glanced up, surprised Andi would knock. She braced herself for an apology, thinking maybe it was Josiah. Her eyes widened to see Dolion facing her instead.

"Hello, I'm sorry if I've startled you, but I just wanted to talk for a moment. I noticed you and Josiah had a bit of an argument, and you seemed very sad."

He walked into the room. Aster wasn't sure how. Her mind suddenly felt muddled. She sat on the bed, and he sat across from her, staring closely into her face.

"I know it's hard to have a falling out with a friend, especially someone you care deeply about," Dolion said with a knowing look.

"I don't know what you mean," Aster said. She did not like his insinuation.

He shrugged. "Well, perhaps I was wrong, but I can tell you are friends. It doesn't do to let yourself stay mad at friends. I'll leave you to go to sleep; I just wanted to make sure you were okay."

Without another word, he gave her a pat on the shoulder and left. Aster felt dazed and uneasy, as if something important had happened, but she'd missed it.

I'm just tired and sad after my fight with Josiah, she thought to herself.

She lay down on the bed and closed her eyes, hoping sleep would welcome her. It did almost immediately. She fell into a deep sleep, rocked by the soft motion of the boat.

All was well.

Then she dreamed.

She glanced around and realized she was on the deck of the boat. Andi and Josiah were talking, and she moved closer to hear what they were saying.

"You know she's not ready, Andi," Josiah said.

"Of course she's not ready. I doubt she's even one of the actual three keys," Andi said.

Aster felt sick to her stomach—how could they be saying this?

"This isn't a memory," she said to herself. "It's just a nightmare." She closed her eyes and tried shaking her head to wake up, but their words only echoed louder in her ears.

When she opened her eyes, she screamed.

A lifeless Josiah lay on the deck of the boat, staring up at her. She ran to him and felt for a pulse. There was none.

"Josiah!" she yelled, shaking him. "Somebody, help!" Aster searched wildly across the boat for help, but it was empty. She was all alone.

"Aster, listen to me," said a voice.

She searched hopelessly for the owner of the voice.

The scene dissolved before her, Josiah disappeared, and faint shadowy figures began forming around her.

"We can't trust Aster," she heard Roark say. "We only need the journal, but I suppose we'll have to take her with us if we don't want her telling the Evanders about us."

"We could try to lose her somewhere in the woods," Josiah's voice replied.

Aster's head twisted in pain as she heard their words, which sounded so true because they manifested the doubts continually nagging at her.

"Aster, listen to me," said the unknown voice a second time, louder than before.

"Who are you?" she cried weakly.

The scene changed, the shadows dissolved, and Aster was facing Dolion. Aster realized she was seeing her exchange with Dolion just hours, or moments, before; she didn't know how long. She watched as Dolion stood up from the table and patted Aster on the shoulder. He used his other and secretly slipped the red leather journal behind his back.

Aster didn't realize she'd left the journal open on the table.

Dolion walked out of the cabin, and as he passed Aster viewing the dream, he turned and looked straight at her.

He can see me, *she thought nervously.*

But how?

"Because I'm not who you think I am," he replied.

Her eyes widened. The world went black.

"No!" she cried out, waking up from the dream. Her hand reached under her pillow, hoping to find the journal there. The journal was gone. Andi had been right; nightmares weren't just nightmares for her.

Her heart dropped, and she pushed herself up, lunged for the door of the cabin, and wrenched it open.

Dolion stood in the middle of the boat, one hand wrapped around Andi's shoulders, and the other holding a knife against her side.

"Aster, whatever is the matter?" he asked in mocked concern. "You didn't have a bad dream, did you?"

"You're a Kasmień, aren't you?" she asked tensely.

He raised his eyebrows in surprise and mock admiration. "Smart girl. I suppose it would have been harder for me to keep hidden the more you learned."

Aster took a step forward, and Dolion tightened his hold on Andi, pushing the tip of the knife closer to her side.

"Stop right there or I'll take her out, like your friend there," Dolion threatened.

Aster gulped, glancing around for Josiah, and saw him lying on the floor, just unconscious, Aster hoped. Yet, the nightmare stuck in her mind, where he lay in the exact spot, dead.

"You have the journal, so why this?" she asked. She was stalling him, but a part of her wanted genuinely to understand what was happening right now.

None of it made sense.

Then, it hit her.

He smiled, watching the realization dawn across her face. "I needed to establish you were the real deal first. It wouldn't do to take Malum the wrong Light Keeper. Once you showed off and ran away with your friend there," he said, nodding towards Josiah's fallen body.

Aster felt like she would be sick. Her instincts in the meadow had been right, the people who attacked them weren't Cu'Sith. They were Kasmiens all along.

"Okay, so if it's me you want, then here I am," she said with feigned confidence.

He shook his head. "You still have to get me through this infernal green tunnel," he said, looking around with a mixture of disgust and something else Aster caught.

Fear. His frantic eyes showed Aster the truth. He feared the Green River.

Clearly, there was one truth among his many lies, she thought to herself.

Dolion believed in the old wives' tales about the Green River.

A plan began forming in her mind.

She needed to act now for her plan to work. She glanced hurriedly at Andi, hoping, she too, had caught on to Dolion's fear.

"What do you want me to do?" Aster yelled, glancing down at Josiah's prone body. "You took out the one person who knew how to travel this river."

"Nice try," Dolion scoffed. "I know you know more than you're letting on. Get us out of this infernal tunnel," he threatened, "or I'll throw her overboard and let the river take her."

His threat didn't scare Aster because she knew Andi could handle the river, plus she knew the tales of the river to be made up.

Bu nodding in agreement to Dolion's demand, she slowly backed up, keeping her eyes locked on Andi.

"Turn around!" he yelled. "I know what you're trying to do!"

Sure you do, Aster thought to herself.

Andi, I have a plan, she projected her thought back toward Andi as she turned around and walked toward the wheel.

She couldn't hear Andi's response without looking at her, but she felt trust and peace emanate from behind her. She smiled to herself. This had been a hurdle she hadn't been able to break yet, feeling a person's emotions when she couldn't look at them.

Josiah's body lay still, but as she went to step over it, she almost screamed. Hoping she hadn't imagined it, she could have sworn he winked at her before returning to his lifeless facade.

You're alive! she thought joyously.

Laughter, that wasn't her own, filled her thoughts. She swallowed back the tears of relief; Josiah had a plan of his own, and she saw it clear as day when she scanned his thoughts; it worked flawlessly with hers.

"Hurry!" Dolion yelled at her.

"I'm trying," she smarted back.

She took the wheel and steered them farther ahead.

It was now or never.

Pushing back a strand of hair, she used the concentration she had created between Andi and Josiah and let go of the control she had just mastered. She kept her eyes on Dolion, trying hard one last time to read his thoughts.

Nice try, she heard him think.

Wait. How— she thought, surprised. If he could answer her, it meant he was once a mind searcher.

Did you imagine I was one of those powerless Evanders' minions, like the Cu-Sith have become?

You won't win! she thought.

What makes you think that? Did your friends here tell you you were something special? That people needed you to save someone who is long dead?

Aster tried breaking their connection but couldn't.

Nice try, but you're not getting rid of me that easily, Dolion thought. *You are nothing. The King and his Knight died long ago, and no legends your friends create will change that.*

Aster… Another voice entered their connection. Aster recognized it as the mysterious one from her nightmare in the cabin.

She felt Dolion's emotions for the first time. Her plan was working.

She grabbed a tighter hold on her thoughts as his end slacked. Something about the mysterious voice gave her a strength and made her less fearful.

Instead of focusing on the situation at hand, she focused on the Vesta. She focused on the stories from Andi, Roark, Mag, and the man surrounded by the children. She focused on the columns Josiah had showed her in the Vesta, specifically the one of the three daughters.

Josiah's voice echoed in her memory. *"The King himself set your purpose. Don't you see it?"*

After the Vesta, she'd continued to doubt, and her nightmare in the cabin didn't help. However, at this moment, something changed.

Aster, go! the unknown voice said.

Her heart stopped, and a smile broke across her face at the wonderful, impossible identity of the mysterious voice.

It was the Knight.

She'd heard it when she read his letter in Mag's garden. She had felt filled with that same strength as she did now.

Dolion's fear continued to grow, which helped Aster confirm her correct deduction.

You can't tell me who I am, she told Dolion through her thoughts.

Impossible— he tried to say with his thoughts, but Aster cut them off. She had full control of their connection now.

I am a daughter of Gaia and Tarron. I am a Light Keeper. I am a Nimus. And you, sir, are no longer welcome on this boat!

Letting go of the control she'd maintained so far, she let the fire inside her break free.

It threw Dolion and Andi off their feet.

Andi pulled free from Dolion and staggered forward, running to Aster. Dolion regained his balance and lunged after her, but Josiah grabbed his ankles and brought him down hard, pinning him to the floor.

Josiah and Dolion fought, and Aster feared Dolion's savagery would be too much for Josiah. Dolion lunged at Josiah with his knife but fell off-balance, giving Josiah the perfect opportunity to push him back into the river. With a large splash, Dolion fell in, eyes full of hatred.

"The journal!" Aster cried out in dismay. She hoped they could have tied him up, then disposed of him, so she could retrieve the journal.

Josiah glanced down where Dolion fell, his face stricken. The realization of what he had done sank in. Andi wrapped her arm around Aster's shaking frame.

"It's okay, it's okay," she soothed.

It was not okay. As Josiah leaned over the boat, a figure surfaced, spitting out water and hissing at the trio on the boat.

Aster felt Andi recoil, and she, too, wanted to turn her head at the sight of what Malum's people really looked like.

Gone were Dolion's chiseled features and dark hair. Dolion's face was covered in red welts, that Aster thought looked like lash marks. Intertwined vines covered in thorns replaced his smooth hair, making his head look like he had stuck it in a rosebush. The one feature that remained the same were his eyes. Aster's felt bile rise in her throat.

"You were there at the school. You led the raid."

He spat out water, gasping for air. "I almost had you that day, if it hadn't been for your meddling friends. At least my people were able to take care of one of them."

"Roark," Aster heard Andi breathe.

"What did you all do to him? Where is he?" Aster yelled down at him.

He just glared at her with pure and unadulterated hatred. "Know this, girl, no matter who you have protecting you, we'll get to you. Malum always gets the last word. He destroyed the King and his precious Knight. Nothing can bring them back. Once he gets his hands on you and the other 'saviors', he'll have what he needs to seal their doom, and yours. And I'll be the one to deliver you into his hands!"

Dolion attempted to swim back to the boat. Josiah prepared to fend him off, but he never got the chance.

Two tree roots from the bank behind Dolion shot out of the ground and straight toward him. They wrapped him up and jerked him backward against the bank with a thud. Dolion's scream echoed through the green tunnel and sent chills down Aster's spine. More roots shot out of the ground from other trees, one hitting the boat so hard it knocked Aster and the others off their feet.

When she stood back up, clinging to the boat to keep steady, she saw the roots pin Dolion's arms back, pulling him into the earth itself till the dirt muffled his cries and his body disappeared from view.

The three of them stood in quiet, faces filled with horror. In the silence, Aster felt water cover her feet, and she looked down in horror to see it filling the boat.

"We're sinking!" she warned the others, realizing one of the tree roots had inadvertently punctured a large hole in their boat.

"What can we do?" Andi asked.

"Ride it out," Josiah said, holding a wound on his arm to stop the bleeding. "Just a little further. Look." He pointed up ahead to the moon, and its glowing light.

Aster realized the tunnel was widening, and they were moving at a rapid pace.

Her face blanched at the sight ahead.

"Josiah!" she yelled over the rushing water.

"Yeah, I know," he replied with forced calm. "It's not as bad as it looks, though."

It looked bad to Aster. The light ahead looked promising, but Aster could only see sky, since the river dropped out just ahead of them.

"A waterfall? You thought this was a good idea?!" she cried.

"It's going to be okay!" He tried to sound positive. "Lay down and put your hands over your chest!" he yelled.

Aster and Andi stared helplessly at each other but braced themselves as instructed.

Aster waited for the ground to fall out beneath them and her stomach to drop with it, but neither happened. Instead, to all their surprise, the boat was being pulled backward. Glancing back, Aster's mouth opened in shock. The roots that had pulled Dolion into the earth were now pulling them to safety.

The roots came from both sides and tightened their grip around the boat. Another root shot out between the others holding the boat and braided itself into a bridge-like structure for the trio to cross carefully to the riverbank. They exchanged confused and shocked glances before venturing out onto the bridge the tree root had created.

Once they were on dry ground, the tree roots released the boat, letting it fall down the water fall and crumble to pieces on impact below.

"That could have been us," Andi stated.

They watched as the tree roots returned to their earthen home, and the woods were silent once again.

"I can't believe that just happened," Aster said in a hollow voice.

"Which part?" Josiah grimaced. "The part where Dolion ended up being one of Malum's creatures? Or the part where the trees came alive and saved us from falling to our deaths?"

"Both," she replied with a shrug. "What do you think he meant by Malum having the last word? How could he use the three keys?"

She didn't expect the other two to answer, but she had to voice the questions gnawing at her now that they were safe.

Andi's legs gave way, and she fell onto the hard earth, laughing uncontrollably. Aster bent to help her but fell as well, causing her to join in the laughter. Josiah stared at them both for a minute before collapsing in a fit of laughter himself. When they caught their breath, Andi studied them with a determined expression, a look Aster had seen before.

She was about to take charge.

"Well then, let's get going. We have a good trek ahead of us."

Josiah and Aster looked at her wide-eyed. Aster could already feel the adrenaline easing out of her system.

Andi stood up and stared down at them, determination etched across her face.

"Andi, don't you think we should rest a minute? Consider the fact there might be more of Malum's creatures waiting for us close by?" Josiah asked, exhausted.

"No, we were just saved by trees. We just survived an attack from a murderous creature hiding right under our noses. We didn't survive all of that to stop now. I suggest we use the moonlight to find a path, head down."

Aster knew it was hopeless to argue with her.

"She's right, Josiah. We can do this. We have to get to Toparius, especially now that we've lost the journal."

The realization that she didn't have her great-grandmother's journal edged in on her, but she couldn't think about it, or she knew she would collapse under the weight of hopelessness that threatened her.

Josiah nodded and got up. He helped Aster up and held on to her hand. "I'm so sorry I let him get away with it, Aster."

She shook her head, not wanting him to take on more guilt. "It's not your fault. You did what you had to do. Besides, he didn't technically get away with it, thankfully. Now it belongs to the trees, I guess."

She gestured to the bank where the roots had dragged Dolion. The image of his hideous face and the sound of his chilling scream stuck in her memory. She knew the scene, would fuel her nightmares for the foreseeable future.

"You'll be fine without it, Aster," Andi comforted. "Remember what your ability is?"

Aster glanced at her quizzically.

Andi sighed. "You can recall things. You can see things in your mind that you have already seen."

Then it clicked, and a smile broke out on Aster's face. "You're right! I have to focus on the journal. I've never done it with something so complicated, but it can't hurt to try. If it works, I should see its pages. Oh, Andi, thank you!"

She gave her a long hug, one they both needed after their ordeal.

Andi held her out at arm's length and looked her and Josiah over.

"Are you two ready to keep going?"

They both nodded and followed Andi as she struck out through the woods. Amazingly, she promptly found them a path. Aster thought the trees were helping them, for their branches seemed to be moving specifically. One minute they were in one spot, and the next they seemed to move aside for the trio to continue walking without difficulty. Aster loved to hike and walk in the woods back home, but even this trek was becoming strenuous for her. She didn't complain. Though. She did,, try to concentrate on her memories of the journal, but it was fuzzy, and images of the river kept interrupting.

The sun was getting low, but they kept walking. Andi told them they could stop for the night, but not long. "We have to travel with as little rest as possible."

They sat down, exhausted and sore from the continuous walking. Aster knew she should sleep, but every time she tried closing her eyes, the scenes with Dolion and the trees played across her vision.

They lay in the silence, surrounded by a guard of trees protecting them. She sensed the other two were also awake.

"So, the tales of the Green River are true." Aster laughed.

"Yes and no," Andi responded. "The stories are true, but it depends on who tries to swim or travel the river. If it's one of pure heart, then they'll be able to swim, travel, float, whatever they want to do. If not… well, you saw what happened."

Aster shuddered. She had undoubtedly seen it, and she figured it would sear across her memory till the day she died.

Aster noticed the trees were leading them toward the edge of the woods, and the canopy above them thinned as the light from the evening sky filtered down on them. They trudged up-hill and down, some paths more treacherous than others. They stopped only for brief breaks, when Aster worked on recalling the contents of the journal. Andi only let them sleep when it became too dark to see. They foraged for food and always found streams just when their water supply became low. Aster was climbing up a steeper hill behind Andi when her foot slipped, and she almost fell, but a tree branch showed up abruptly within reach from a nearby tree. She felt thankful for whatever magic filled these woods.

On their fourth night, Aster wondered how much longer they had to travel, especially in these woods. She felt they would never find their way out of this maze of trees and trails. She began to wonder if the trees really had good intentions or if they were just luring them into a trap. Andi relieved her fears the next night as they were lying down for a few hours' rest.

"If I'm right," Andi said, "we should reach Toparious tomorrow morning or early afternoon."

"Really?" Aster asked. Every part of her ached—her mind, body, and spirit. She was also running out of paper from Josiah's pack, which he'd saved. She'd resorted to writing in extraordinarily small letters to fit in what she could remember from the journal.

"Andi…" Aster wondered how to ask something that had been nagging at her.

"Yes?"

"What if… the Academy…?"

"What if the Academy is destroyed, or the Evanders have taken over it?" Andi asked.

Aster sighed and nodded. She hated thinking the worst, but she also wanted a plan.

"There are safe houses on the outskirts of the city," Andi explained. "They're large enough to house anyone who survived. We made them when the storms began growing closer and the Evanders began blaming us for them."

"Why would they blame us?" Aster asked.

"The Divums can manipulate the weather and create storms; therefore, they have become the scapegoats. We've researched the storms, though, and they aren't coming from Light Keepers. At least, they aren't coming from any reputable Light Keepers.

"The Academy leaders realized the day would come when the Evanders would force them to stop teaching Light Keepers. Every day, life became less safe for Light Keepers. They created the safe-houses to be nondescript but exceedingly capable of what they would require to continue their work."

"Like Mag's?" Aster asked, putting the pieces together.

Andi nodded. "Mag's house is more like a halfway house, because it's so far from the Academy. Nevertheless, it's helped many traveling across Veridi."

"I hope the Academy is still there," she said. "I want you to see it. Especially the library. You'll love the library."

Aster laughed, and soon she drifted off to sleep, falling into various dreams.

One dream had her walking through the woods in a perpetual circle until she wanted to scream in frustration. In another dream, she walked out of the woods and stepped into a bright light.

The light dimmed. She saw the same beautiful vista she had seen in her dreams before, the one from the painting. This time the Academy reflected the light off its many windows. She strained her eyes, but it kept looking farther and farther away. She took a step forward to get closer, when the sky darkened, casting a dark cloud over the beautiful view. A chill swept over her, and in the distance, she could hear screaming.

Dolion's screaming.

The river below her turned black, and she saw the tree roots shooting up out of the ground, snaking their way up towards her. They wrapped themselves around her ankles and pulled her down. She screamed and tried clawing her way back up, but they just kept pulling her down, down into black nothingness, her ears filling with the sound of Dolion's screams.

"Aster, wake up!" Josiah called out.

She woke up thrashing, sweat pouring down her face and neck, her heart beating faster than a hummingbird's wings.

"It's okay, Aster. You're okay," Josiah said quietly, one arm wrapped around her shoulders and the other pushing her damp hair out of her face.

"What happened?" she mumbled.

"You were having a nightmare," Andi said, looking at her with concern.

Aster put her hand to her forehead and groaned.

"It didn't start out as a nightmare. I dreamed of the Academy, and this time I saw the Academy itself…"

"And then what?" Josiah asked.

Aster just shook her head. She didn't want to replay what she had just seen. She saw Andi sensed what she'd dreamed was more a nightmare. A sick feeling filled Aster as she realized what she might have just witnessed in her dream was what Roark had feared. Andi's warning about her nightmares returned, and she began shaking in fear.

"It could just be a dream…" she said, hoping she sounded more reassured than she felt

Andi hung her head. "A mind searcher's dreams are never just a dream."

"We won't know for sure until we get there," Josiah whispered.

Chapter 15

They started out on what they hoped was the last leg of their journey. According to Andi, they should leave the Green Forest soon and see Toparius not long after. They walked in silence, each pondering the potential reality of Aster's nightmare.

Aster felt guilty for telling them, especially Andi. She could feel Andi's concern, fear, and sadness, and it exhausted her. They didn't stop walking, though Josiah and Aster fell back. Andi pushed ahead, and Aster could feel her desperation to discover the fate of her friends and the Academy.

The tall, helpful, green-barked trees of the Green Forest gave way to smaller pines and white oaks.

They began walking up an incline, Andi running now.

She stopped at the top, and Aster and Josiah joined her a moment later, panting, trying to catch their breaths.

Aster squinted against the morning light as they followed Andi around a small bend and walked out of the woods into a large clearing that slopped downward into the town.

"Welcome to Toparius," Andi proudly declared.

Toparius, sprawled out below them, with houses and buildings big and small scattered across the open land. Aster thought they looked like doll houses from their vantage point. Little streets wove across the flat valley. A wall surrounded the outskirts of the town, separating it from the forest on the outside. She saw smoke rising from the chimneys; the town was waking up. The sight made her smile. Perhaps it was because they were reaching the end of their journey. Despite having yet to step foot in the village or meet the people she had a feeling inside her, she would find her answers here.

Her eyes followed one street and saw merchants walking down it, and to her surprise, she thought she saw a glimmer of light.

"I love it," she said.

"It's grown since the last time I saw it," Josiah commented.

"Is that the ocean?" Aster asked Andi, pointing oast the merchant pushing his cart down the street out of view.

"Yes, it is. The port faces Vela. The village looks the same, but the outskirts have tripled in size. It's full of strong, proud, and resilient people. They struggle like we all do under the Evanders, but they handle it well. Overall, I think you'll find them quite welcoming. Though, we won't have time to linger. The storms thankfully haven't touched it yet, but I don't know how much longer that will last."

Aster and Josiah followed Andi down the hill and through a dense forest of trees, where they hit a path that led them straight into the town. On their way, they passed clusters of houses scattered around, a farm, and eventually the city itself.

Aster saw a school and a bustling marketplace. Andi spun around and pulled Aster's hood up, as well as her own, before they went farther.

"Just in case," she said. Aster watched, impressed, as Andi walked with purpose yet casually enough so as not to draw attention.

"This city is so different from Verd," Aster said. She watched the people milling around, smiling, trading stories, and selling goods. They looked happy. They weren't glancing over their shoulders. They didn't act fearful of who or what might be watching. The Evanders had evidently found the people of Toparius not easily corruptible. She decided that had to be a reason they'd moved the capital to Venari.

A delicious smell wafted from a nearby tavern, hitting Aster with a wave of hunger. Her stomach growled, and she winced as Josiah looked at her with wide, laughing eyes.

"Stop it," she laughed, pushing him.

"It's nothing to be embarrassed about," he laughed back. "Your stomach is just saying what we're all feeling."

Andi stopped and looked at them with a grimace. "He's right. I'm sorry I've kept us on such a hard schedule. I just want to know the state of the Academy and everyone there."

Aster also sensed Andi still hoped they would find the Academy in one piece.

"Let's go in here and grab a bite to eat," Andi suggested, leading them to the tavern producing the delightful smells.

Inside, they found a large, friendly, and noisy crowd eating, laughing, and talking. The tables were full, but Josiah located one in a back corner. They wove their way through the crowd, receiving some stares, but none of them unfriendly or hostile.

"Thankfully, with the harbor a few miles away, Toparius is used to strangers," Andi muttered, keeping her head down.

"What can I getch'a?" An older woman with kind eyes and a warm smile appeared at their table.

"Whatever food you would recommend, we will eat," Andi replied.

"Ah, I love hungry customers!" The woman laughed.

Aster liked her laugh. It was warm and full, and she realized how nice it felt to be around people again. It hadn't occurred to her, but it had been almost two weeks since she and Josiah had left Cedrus. She missed Flora and Collin and their children, especially sweet Morgan. She sensed Josiah and Andi relaxing and feeling at ease in the tavern as well.

The lady with the warm laughter brought them plates piled with a food a little while later and large mugs of something refreshing. They ate in silence, fueling to finish the journey. Between bites, Aster wrote on her scrap of paper. She jumped as a hand appeared in front of her, holding a small notebook.

She glanced up, and the woman smiled down at her. "I thought you might need this. It looks like you've 'bout run out of room there."

Aster took the notebook and smiled back. "Thank you so much..."

"Sarah," she replied. "And who might you and your weary group be?"

"We're very thankful for your hospitality and kindness," Andi answered, careful not to give Aster a look for almost revealing their identity to a stranger.

Sarah seemed to understand their desire for privacy and nodded. "Well, if you need anything, just ask."

"I'm sure she's as genuine as she seems," Andi whispered as she walked away. "But we need to stay on our guards."

Aster nodded, and they continued to eat while she spent more time writing as quickly as the memories came to her.

They finished eating, left Sarah a generous tip, and slipped out the side door into the fading twilight.

"How much farther?" Aster asked. She looked at the darkening sky with concern.

Andi sighed. "It should just be a couple miles from the edge of town. It's hidden, so I'm not sure if we should wait till morning when we'll have enough light or risk trying to find it in the dark."

"We need to get there tonight. Waiting here will give more opportunity for someone to discover us," Josiah commented.

"You're constantly trying to do tasks immediately instead of correctly," said a voice behind them.

They all spun around.

Andi put her arm out to shield Aster and Josiah, Josiah's hand went to his knife, and Aster tried focusing on the dark figure standing in the alley's shadow, to see if she could read their thoughts.

She gasped and put her hand on Andi's shoulder. They weren't in any danger.

"It's Roark," she said.

Andi gasped but didn't run to him until he stepped out of the shadows and lowered his hood. Aster noticed his face bore scratches, and he held himself at a slant, as if he'd injured one of his legs.

"What, didn't you expect to see me here?" Roark laughed as he and Andi shared a warm embrace.

Aster and Josiah turned their heads, giving their friends as much of a private reunion as possible.

Roark release Andi, and he motioned for the other two to join them. He clapped a hand on Josiah's shoulder and looked at him proudly.

"You did well," he said. "You not only got Aster here safely, but you evidently saved Andi. Thank you, Josiah."

Josiah seemed taken aback by his mentor's gratitude and pride in him, but it impressed Aster he didn't puff up at the praise. Instead, she felt his humility and joy at knowing Roark was alive.

Roark held out a hand to Aster, who took it, and her heart ached, for she could feel the pain he had experienced still filling his thoughts.

"I'm all right," he said, realizing she was reading him. "I'm even better now knowing you have made it this far. You seem exhausted but stronger," he commented, staring at her.

She nodded. "I'm exhausted, but I'm glad there's a part of me that seems stronger. I'm so glad you're okay."

"It's all thanks to you," Roark replied.

She and the others looked at him.

He laughed. "To keep a long story short, you did something that woke up the trees. They started spreading out, or that's what it looked like, and light spilled into the forest. Whatever creatures my captors were, they didn't like the light. They became so disoriented by it that the one holding me let go and I slipped away. I arrived here last night."

Aster knew the moment when Roark was talking about. The trees had come to their rescue when they were in need, when Dolion threatened them, and when they almost fell to their death. It must have awakened them to Roark's plight as well. Aster felt immensely grateful for the Green Forest, despite the horrors she had witnessed there.

"The creatures are Malum's, Roark," Josiah answered Roark's question about his captors. "I'm not sure precisely what they are, but they are his followers. We had a run in with one of them ourselves."

Roark gave a concerned glance at Andi, but she shook her head. "We're fine. We worked together and took of it, and the trees did the rest, she said with a grimace and shudder."

Roark kept a concerned look on his face and shook his head. "I'm glad you all eliminated the creature, but this is troubling news. We don't know where Malum is or what his creatures actually are. And the fact they can disguise themselves—"

Andi placed a hand up to stop him. "Roark, we can't answer those questions now. Right now, we're together, and we're only a few miles from safety."

He nodded in reluctant agreement but looked up at the darkening sky as the sun gradually fell. "We shouldn't be out here when it's dark. We'll rest tonight, then leave for the Academy at first light."

They all agreed, even Josiah. Aster read his thought, and could tell he would not balk at Roark's plans again.

At least for right now.

"Where can we stay?" Aster asked.

They glanced around, hoping a place would pop out at them.

"All of my contacts are closer to the sea," Andi said. "That's more than a mile from here, which puts us farther away from the Academy tomorrow morning."

Aster just started feeling the chains of hopelessness wrap themselves around her when a voice startled them from behind.

"So sorry." Sarah stood at the back door. She held the money they'd left in her hand. "I came out to catch you and give this back. It's too much for people who evidently need it. Now, though," she said, putting her hands on her hips as she surveyed the tired group, "I'm thinking you also need somewhere safe and out of sight to rest your head."

They looked questioningly at each other. They felt wary to trust a stranger, but a roof over their heads sounded wonderful.

Roark opened his mouth, but she held up her hands.

"Listen, my house is at the edge of town; you can't miss it. There's a barn in the back. You're welcome to sleep in the loft for the night. You'll find blankets and pillows up there. I keep it fixed up for folk who need a place to stay—or hide."

Without another word, she returned Andi's money, and walked back to the tavern, shutting the door behind her.

Roark looked at Aster. "Could you read her at all?"

"Yes," Aster replied, "and I get the sense that we can trust her."

Roark nodded, and they all agreed it stood as their only option. They walked hurriedly through city, taking the least visible routes when possible, trying to beat the dark. The houses and buildings became fewer the closer they came to the surrounding wall. They ultimately reached the edge of the city and saw a modest-size home with a large barn out behind it, just as Sarah had told them. They also understood why she told them, *"You can't miss it."*

A grove of trees with lanterns hanging in them surrounded the house. The lantern lights gave off a beautiful glow, like the trees were home to a host of fireflies. Aster couldn't keep her mouth from dropping open in amazement. The house and its surroundings gave off the air of magic she had felt at Mag's.

The lantern light provided showed them their way back to the barn with ease. They discovered the blankets and pillows and settled down to sleep.

Aster struggled to close her eyes for the longest time, despite having felt exhausted on their walk here. She realized that tomorrow they would reach the Academy, no matter what state they found it in. She felt like no matter what happened, she would receive answers.

Aster was lying near the loft's door, which she left cracked open. She got up and pushed it open a little farther, looking up at the stars and taking in the beautiful trees full of lanterns surrounding Sarah's property. Out of the corner of her eye, she saw a figure approaching the house, but before Aster could become frightened, she realized it was Sarah. Sarah plodded slowly to her house, but Aster sensed she possessed an air of strength. Sarah paused to look back at the barn. Aster didn't know if the woman saw her, but she waved just in case. She concentrated on Sarah to see if she could read her.

Be safe, she heard Sarah's thoughts resonate in the space between them.

Aster kept herself from gasping outloud. It wasn't just that she could hear Sarah's thoughts, but she could tell Sarah had directed them straight to her.

Before she could do or think anything else, Sarah went inside, and Aster felt the exhaustion return to her body and her eyes become heavy. She kept the door open, and the bright stars and soft glowing trees were the last things she saw before sleep claimed her.

Roark woke them all up early the next morning, ready to get moving. Aster wanted to see if Sarah was home so they could thank her, but Roark said it was best they leave promptly and secretly.

"He's right, Aster," Andi said as they started out, their backs to the farm and the bustling little town. "She knows we're grateful for what she did. Besides, it's time we finish this part of the journey, don't you think?"

They walked in pairs at first, Andi and Roark conversing softly as Josiah and Aster took up the rear.

"I still can't believe we're almost there," Aster mused to Josiah.

"It seems like it's been a long time coming," he replied.

"Not for me. I feel like this has all happened so quickly."

"Not for me," he stated. "Since Roark realized you were the one, I was ready to come back. This place is my home, and I forgot how much I loved it there. The mission to find you has been my longest. I didn't realize how much I'd miss the Academy."

"Well, I just hope I'm the right one," she muttered.

He gave her an exasperated look.

"Just kidding!" She laughed. "I know this is my journey, but it's still hard to grasp sometimes. I'm so close to finding answers to the millions of questions I have left."

To her surprise, Josiah gently took her hand in his as they continued to walk. He said nothing and kept looking ahead. It gave her a sense of confidence and reminded her she wasn't alone in this.

"No matter what we find, everything you've gone through has shown this is your purpose," he whispered.

She felt tears brimming in her eyes, but she didn't want him to see his words had made her cry. Instead, she fixed her gaze on the fluffy clouds above and squeezed his hand in appreciation.

Aster could tell when they were getting closer to the Academy because Andi's pace increased, as well as Roark's. Aster and Josiah did their best to keep up with them, and with each step, Aster's nerves grew. She wanted to find the Academy intact and full of welcoming arms. She also worried that if it was still standing, the people there wouldn't accept her.

Their path sloped downward, fortunately less treacherous than what they'd experienced in the Green Forest. The slope leveled, and they came to the base of a cliff.

Andi stopped and stared up at it, and Aster could feel her emotions of fear and anticipation.

Roark gave her a gentle push and led them onto a narrow path, stopping abruptly at the base of the cliff. Ivy cascaded down the side, and Aster wondered why they just stood here staring at it. However, Roark and the others weren't deterred, and Roark pushed back the ivy, revealing a low tunnel.

Josiah nodded to Aster, still holding her hand.

"Come on, we're almost there."

She let him lead her through the tunnel, ducking her head. She thought the darkness would swallow them as she let the ivy curtain drop behind her, but light still filled the tunnel from an open passage ahead of them. They reached the tunnel's exit and stepped out into the morning sun.

Aster gasped, and Andi let out a cry of relief. The Academy was still standing and looked untouched by any evil forces. Aster felt overwhelmed with relief and awe that she was ultimately seeing it in real life.

The rolling hills, the river that flowed into a lake. The tree groves, lush green grass that sparkled with the morning dew; it was her dream come to life. And the Academy—it was still standing.

"Oh, Roark, it's all still here. The Academy," Andi cried. "Do you think everyone is okay?"

He smiled confidently. "Let's go find out."

They followed a worn path through the tree groves, up the hills, and across a bridge over the sparkling lake. The path changed to stone and led to an enormous, castle-like mansion.

The Academy.

People milled around outside. Andi sighed and ran the rest of the way. The others jogged to catch up with her, and Aster noticed people had started coming out of the mansion. They must have realized who had arrived.

An older woman caught Andi in a hug. A group of men, young and old, greeted Roark. People continued to emerge, and Aster could tell many were just starting their morning.

"Josiah!" a young boy cried out. Josiah ran to meet him, sweeping him up in a bear hug, laughing.

Aster stayed behind, watching the joyful reunions, and missing her family so much it hurt. She didn't know where they were.

Andi wiped away her tears and looked over at Aster standing off by herself. Aster watched her ask the woman something before coming over to her.

"Aster," she said with a smile.,"there are people who'd like to see you."

Aster nodded and geared herself up to meet these people who would put their trust in her to help them. However, Andi led her past the woman, Roark, and Josiah, straight to a group standing off by themselves, looking around frantically.

Aster's heart stopped.

It was her family.

Leaving Andi behind, she ran straight for them, tears streaming down her face. They were safe. They were here!

All except her father.

"Momma!" she cried as she fell into her mother's arms.

"Oh, Aster, I'm so sorry! Can you ever forgive me?"

Aster looked up at her, tears blurring her vision. "For what?"

"For not telling you the truth. I was wrong. I knew your father was wrong, and I did nothing. I used the excuse I didn't know how to teach what you needed. And I wanted to trust he knew best. I let fear and doubt take over me." Her mother's voice caught on a sob.

Aster wiped away her mother's tears, then her own.

"It's okay, Momma. I know you tried. It's okay."

They held each other, sobbing with relief and regret. They stood like this for a few moments before Aster gave her brothers and sister each a hug, happy to see them despite the past.

"We were wrong to treat you like we did, Aster," Amity said, hanging her head. "Can you ever forgive us?" she cried.

Aster instantly wanted to say yes, but a piece of her heart still stung, broken by their actions.

"I forgive you, but it will take a while for me to forget."

Her sister nodded.

"But I'm going to try," Aster added, lifting her sister's face to look at her. She turned back to her mother. "Where's Father?" she asked.

Her mother shook her head and avoided her eyes. "He's just too afraid. I think he let fear and doubt fill him so much he couldn't find a way to break free."

Aster tried to keep more tears from flowing, but a few traitors escaped, like pieces of her heart chipping away. Before she could focus on her father's absence too long, Andi came over and pulled her away.

"You need to come and meet someone," she said, leading Aster inside the Academy itself. Aster's head swiveled around, trying to take it all in. From the beautiful marble floors beneath her feet to the vaulted ceilings above her head, Aster felt overwhelmed by the beauty. Andi led her up a grand set of stairs, down a long corridor, eventually stopping at a large pair of double oak doors. Andi knocked once and went inside, Aster following close behind.

Aster's eyes felt like they could pop out of her head as they entered the largest library she had ever seen in her entire life. Two floors of bookshelves lined every inch of the room. Light flooded the room from the floor-to-ceiling windows. The light reflected off the gold-leaf bindings on many of the books.

"I knew you'd like it." Andi laughed, watching Aster take in her surroundings.

"Like it?" Aster said. "I even think I could have dreamed this."

"I'm glad you think so!" said a lilting voice from above.

Aster watched as a striking figure came walking down the circular staircase. Her red hair was brighter than Aster's own locks and braided neatly down her back. Aster felt underdressed and acutely aware she needed a bath when she saw the woman's clean-cut outfit and polished face.

"Aster," Andi said, "this is Levine. She's in charge of the Veridi Academy. Levine, this is Aster."

Aster wiped her dirty hands discreetly against her even dirtier clothes, before shaking Levine's smooth, clean hands.

It's nice to meet you, Aster.

Aster almost jumped, because Levine had just talked to her telepathically.

"You're a Nimus, too?" Aster asked aloud.

"Yes, I am." Levine laughed. "Most of us here are Nimuses. With a few exceptions," she added with a glance at Andi. "But I think you're one of the most important mind searchers I have met. According to Mag, you're one of the three keys to finding the Knight," Levine said, motioning them to join her at the large table with maps and books spread out across it.

Aster took a deep breath and nodded. "I am."

She could feel Andi's pride and joy radiating throughout her thoughts. This was the first time Aster had admitted it out loud.

"Wonderful!" Levine said with a clap of her hands. "We can't waste any more time in finding the others. I think it's high time Ignis is reunited, don't you?"

"Yes," Aster said, feeling rallied by Levine's positivity. "Where do we look?" she asked.

"Well, I believe we've found a logical solution to this," Levine said, motioning to the maps and papers. "We know we're looking for descendants of Gaia and Tarron, and each of their daughters was born with a unique ability. Since we have our Nimus," she said, nodding at Aster, "we're going to search through Divums and Quarriers next. We'll send a few of our Light Keepers with the news to those in Gemma and Vela. Hopefully, we can search through the records they have, and we'll find a lead to our final two. Your great-grandmother's journal is going to help tremendously."

Aster's face fell. "I'm so sorry, but we lost the journal on the Green River… I tried to write what I could remember, though," Aster added, reaching for the notebook in her pocket.

Levine's face sagged a little, her excitement deflating. But Aster watched her eyes light up as if she had just remembered something miraculous.

"Wait right here!" Levine told them. She hurried nimbly to a built-in cabinet beneath the shelves in the back corner. She pulled something off the shelf and hurried back to them.

"Here," she said happily.

"How…" Aster asked, stunned as she looked at a perfect copy of her lost journal.

"They instructed every Light Keeper to keep two copies of their journals; one copy stays with them and the other stays at their respective Academy. That was your great-grandmother's copy of her original."

Aster realized this was the journal she saw her great-grandfather writing in before the Cu-Sith killed him.

"Aster," Levine said kindly. "Aster, we will help you as much as possible while you're here. Unfortunately, you don't have as much time as I'd like. But I don't' doubt you can do it!"

Aster nodded, straightening her shoulders. "I can, and I will."

"Good." Levine smiled. "Now, I believe someone is waiting in the hallway to show you to your room. Tomorrow we will begin your training."

Andi gave her a hug before sending her off. "I'll see you again soon," she whispered.

Aster briefly read her thoughts and wondered why Andi thought she would be leaving Veridi soon. She sighed, exhausted mentally and physically, and wanting to sleep. Aster opened the doors and smiled. She wasn't surprised at who was waiting for her.

"There you are," Josiah said, acting as if he had been waiting hours.

"Well, I'm sorry to have kept someone so important waiting. You're taking me to my room?"

"I know this place like the back of my hand. And if you're not nicer to me, I'll have to move your room to the basement."

She rolled her eyes and followed him up the stairs to the third floor.

"So, you met Levine?" he asked.

"Yes, I like her. She said I'll start training tomorrow," Aster replied, yawning as she did.

"I bet you'll sleep well tonight," Josiah said as they stopped at her room.

"I'm sure I'll fall asleep the minute my head hits the pillow."

He laughed. "Do you think you can stay awake for a little while longer? I'd like to show you my favorite spot here."

She looked at his eyes, gazing intensely into hers.

It suddenly felt like she could stay awake for hours.

"Show me," she said.

He led her to a hidden door on the third floor, revealing a set of stairs leading to the attic.

"Your favorite spot is the attic?" she asked.

Josiah rolled his eyes. "Not even close."

He led her to a small side door, slid the lock open, and pushed the door outward. He turned and held out his hand to her, helping her out onto the roof.

"This is my favorite spot," he said, gesturing out in front of them.

Aster realized none of her dreams could ever capture this beautiful view. The sun shone high above them, and Aster could see every inch of the hidden valley separating the Academy from the city of Toparius. From this height, she could even see the ocean, sparkling like diamonds.

"Thank you, Josiah," she said sincerely.

"For what?" he asked.

"For everything, for showing me your favorite spot. For helping me accept my place in all this, being there for me when I needed you, and always encouraging my daydreams instead of thinking I was crazy."

He took her hand. "I've never thought you're not crazy. I just didn't care if you were or not. Everything crazy about you is what I like best."

Her heart thudded, her cheeks grew warm, and her stomach fluttered with a million butterfly wings.

She looked back out at the beautiful view before. "I guess that's how I know I can count on you, then," she said, leaning her head on his strong shoulder.

"You can always count on me, Aster. No matter what's up ahead."

She sighed, feeling happier than she could ever remember. Here she sat on the roof of the Academy, having left home, and traveled across Veridi; it all felt so impossible to her. In that time, she'd learned more about herself than she could have ever imagined.

Aster felt in her bones that, for now, everything was going to be okay. Her family and friends surrounded her, she'd found her purpose, and she felt safe to be herself, which was a new feeling for her. Tomorrow, she'd start working on finding the answers that would help her become what she needed.

Acknowledgements

Mom, you have always encouraged my love of and writing. You taught me to cultivate my creativity, and I'm so glad to call you my best friend.

Annie, you're the best sister I could ask for, and you're always my Cheerleader.

Lincoln, I can't wait for you to read this one day. I love watching you grow, and I hope your curiosity never dies.

Nana and Bum. Nana, thank you for taking me to the library and reading to me on the swing. Bum, thank you for your legacy of faith, I miss you every day. And everyone else who has cheered me on and encouraged me in writing.

To my 5th period seventh graders, thanks for your help in recreating the cover of this reprint. You all constantly keep me on my toes.